Into The Sun

Susan Draper

Published by Susan Draper, 2023.

This is a work of fiction. Similarities to real people, places, or events are entirely coincidental.

INTO THE SUN

First edition. September 19, 2023.

Written by Susan Draper.

This story is dedicated to those who believe in that which lies not beneath, but beyond. Keep reaching for the stars.

Chapter One-Liftoff

Planet Earth shakes underneath the huge thrusters of the rocket ship. Within the cramped forward flight deck, which towers a mind-boggling 500 feet above ground zero, Commander Olivia Newman reviews a hologram screen in front of her. To the common layman, it would be gibberish but to her trained eye, it makes sense. All systems display a green check mark. Only seconds remain before she and her primarily rookie crew will be slammed back in their reclined seats, hot breath taken away as adrenalin-infused blood rushes to support internal organs.

"Quantum One, you are cleared for liftoff." Mission control communicates the final confirmation.

Olivia glances at her assistant command pilot, Nick Johansen. His gloved fingers clutch the arms of the seat slightly harder, but the reassuring look he sends his commanding officer helps to maintain her unwavering composure. They've done this before on three prior lunar missions.

"Copy that." Nick's voice shakes from the force of the incredible power coursing through his body. He braces for departure.

Behind him, three additional astronauts sit in the mid module of the massive rocket. Systems engineer Devon McDonald, Chief Medical Officer Dr. Susan Dorfmeyer, and mission specialist, Veronica Cortez, anxiously await with pounding hearts. This is their first launch. What little saliva they had in their mouths is long gone as they listen to the countdown coming through their headsets. The months of rigorous training they completed are about to be tested.

"Ten, nine, eight, seven, six, five, four, three, two, one. Liftoff!"

Incredible g-force sucks them back with relentless power, as if they just received a punch to the solar plexus. Intense pressure inside their spacesuit helmets increases to maximum levels. Additional oxygen flows in to supplement deep inhalations. Biometric readings flash on the inside of helmet visors, assuring the crew their hearts are somehow still beating. Far below, inside mission control's sprawling headquarters, hundreds of analysts monitor every last piece of data, the launch stages progressing like well-rehearsed scenes of a play.

This one hundredth mission, occurring in the present year of 2200, will transport the crew to low-Earth orbit. From there, the rocket transitions to a nuclear propulsion system. This provides necessary speed and power for the second and final stage of their journey, culminating in a parachute-assisted landing near the Mars International Village of Space Scientists, IVOSS, for short. The community is run by Earth's most advanced space programs who have formed a peaceful coalition on the red planet with one goal in mind. Expanding exploration of the universe. At least this is what the press releases claim.

"Congratulations, Quantum One. Reporting a successful launch. Please prepare for transition to direct fusion drive propulsion." Cheers are heard from mission control. The crew breathes a little easier as the g-force diminishes to a more tolerable level.

Commander Olivia smiles at Nick before responding to mission HQ.

"Thanks, Houston. Reporting all systems optimal. Preparing for DDP." She switches to crew only comms.

"Veronica, Devon, Susan-how are you doing back there? Any strange sensations in your pants?"

"Not yet, Commander, but I came close to it." Devon laughs and so do the others. "Somehow, those launch simulators don't do justice to the real thing. That was nothing short of fucking amazing. Pardon the language, Commander."

"Yes, we still get pumped over it, too. Each and every time. And I told you all. You can speak freely around me. The occasional swear word is fine." Nick smiles at Olivia's reminder. They share a special bond. Both graduated from the United States Naval Academy and were selected at the same time for NASA's Planetary Mission Program. Either one would have been an excellent choice to commandeer the latest journey. As fate would have it, Olivia was selected. It hasn't affected their professional or even personal relationship in the least. They fit together. Plain and simple. Nick is recently divorced. Olivia is still looking for Mr. Right. Now that Nick is single again, well, that changes everything. Maybe it's time to move forward.

Dr. Dorfmeyer reaches for the crucifix around her neck, temporarily forgetting it's covered by the spacesuit. She is an attractive, thirty-year-old family practitioner and holds a PhD in reproductive studies. Her very supportive husband, Gary, has agreed to work remotely so he can watch their two preschool kids while Susan follows her dream of traveling to Mars. Pangs of guilt hit when she dwells on how long they will be separated from each other. The memory of her kids' anguished pleas to stay closer to home fill her head, bringing a sharp sting to her eyes. Little Zoe had flung her small arms around Susan's neck, sniveling into her chest the morning she departed for training camp. Her older brother, James, tried to be brave but his lower lip trembled when she kissed him goodbye. Susan had almost capitulated but the allure of co-managing the ever-challenging healthcare needs of an interplanetary mission was too much. Her childhood dreams are being realized.

Thanks to her persistence in the application process, the doctor has been selected to help manage the health of her crewmates, along with fellow colonized citizens of IVOSS. The mission length was not entirely clarified when she interviewed. Although the return trip duration to Earth has been shortened to one month, she expects she'll remain away from her family for at least a year. It will all be worth it, she reminds herself. Still, it's going to be the hardest thing she's ever done.

Systems engineer, Devon, thinks about his fiancé Nicole, for a few seconds. Sometimes he wonders if getting engaged was the right thing to do. He decided to propose three months ago, even though they'd only been dating around a year. Nicole said yes, but there was a slight hesitation before she answered. He senses she is still withholding some type of information from him. Devon figures it's just his overactive brain planting unwarranted seeds of doubt. His mom and dad love Nicole. She has a steady job in fashion design. Plus, he's not getting any younger. Nicole satisfies him sexually. All the one-night stands were great when he was in college but there's more to life than a quick lay with a hot girl. Sex can be just as hot, hell, even hotter, when you're familiar with your partner. Devon chuckles at the memory of their last night together when they made love on the hood of his Camaro.

Sweet night that was.

He jerks himself back to the present, scanning several instrument panels.

Veronica Cortez, mission specialist, brings her vast amount of geological knowledge to IVOSS. She is currently considered one of the leading experts in regolith management and hydroponic plant growth. She'll be bringing some innovative ideas to increase crop production. She goes by V, and prides herself on being the only girl in her family to pursue a higher education. Her mom, a divorcee, worked two jobs after her husband left, when V was only ten years old. V knows she wouldn't be where she is today if it wasn't through the efforts of the one woman who always has her back. It was hard not having a father around, but her mom made sure V had a home to return to. After school. After a night shift slinging burgers. After her loss of virginity to a classmate who decided to move on to another girl a week later. Life could suck sometimes.

"My door will always be open to you, V. You're my whole world. No matter how bad things get, just remember, you can come home if necessary. I'll do my best to turn things around."

V had gotten her grades up and applied to several colleges. Slowly but surely her fortune improved, largely fueled by the supportive encouragement of her mom. When she received her college degree both of them cried. V knew she wasn't done making her mom proud.

Chapter Two-Contact

"DDP initiation confirmed. Finalizing trajectory. Happy Sailing, Commander." Mission control sends confirmation Q-One is full steam ahead to reach the international landing zone of Mars.

"Copy that. We all felt the thrust. What's the most up to date ETA?" Olivia asks the question everyone wants to know.

"We estimate an arrival in approximately 30 days, Commander. You have enough supplies onboard to double that number. All prior missions have arrived ahead of schedule."

"Thanks for the information, Houston. We—

"Quantum One, Quantum One, we seem to have lost communication. Please provide status."

"Q-One, Q-One. Do you copy?"

Commander Olivia tries to respond but her words come out with no sound. The interior of the space craft is filled with bright light. She brings her hands up over her face, squinting in the harsh glare.

"Quantum One, what's going on there? Requesting immediate communication with mission control."

Static, low and soft, comes through the operators' headsets. Heads are turned to each other, in confusion. It's like someone is tuning a radio station too far out of signal range. High-tech video feeds display nothing but snowy screens. Something is seriously wrong.

"Quantum One, we've lost video comms along with audio. Please advise immediately."

Inside mission headquarters on Earth, every single employee realizes it must be grave if zero astronaut comms are being received. The only data they're receiving is coming from the rocket. All systems are optimal as the spacecraft continues to catapult toward the Martian surface. But, what about the commander and her crew?

The light within the module returns to a normal level. Olivia can barely make out the shape of something floating in front of her. Her mouth drops open in awe when she sees it's a face with two huge, black eyes and vertical slits for a nose. There is no mouth. A shimmery, vague outline of some kind of body hangs below the head, floating in and out of her vision.

Jesus Christ, what the hell is that? A million questions flood Olivia's head.

Am I dreaming? A few seconds ago, I was talking to someone. Who was it? Shit, I seem to be having trouble remembering details. My name is Olivia Newman. I'm on a Mars mission. We are en route but—

A masculine voice speaks to her telepathically, interrupting jumbled thoughts and decreasing comprehension.

I am Mithra. Do not be afraid. I come from Star Rejenitus. Reji have lived there for billions of years. Your craft has been tethered to us and your male crew members have been placed in sleep mode. They will recall nothing of what is about to transpire. You and the other two females will be taken aboard our vessel for, how should I describe it...an intervention.

The creature has no eyelids. The way it's staring at Olivia makes her quite uncomfortable. She closes her own eyes for a second or two, hoping whoever or whatever this is will be gone when she opens them again. No dice, it's still there. She looks to her right and sees Nick is out cold, his head slumped down on his chest. Olivia notices he is breathing deeply and steadily. Behind her, Devon is out, too. Susan and Veronica appear to be in some kind of hypnotic state. Their eyes are open, but they stare straight ahead.

Olivia opens her mouth to send them a direct comm but, again, she's unable to hear her own words. It succeeds in freaking her out even more.

This has got to be the most fucked up scenario I've ever been a part of.

Olivia takes a few deep inhalations to calm her frazzled nerves. She's starting to get a headache.

We will communicate telepathically in your native language. This is the only method utilized by Reji. I can decipher your thoughts, although precise comprehension of them, may, at times, be difficult.

Mithra's eyes bore into Olivia's.

The spacecraft you command has crossed paths with our own solar vessel. We want to use your female bodies for a special mission.

Olivia stares back in disbelief. Whatever this thing is, it obviously has the ability to force humans into various states of consciousness.

Over my dead body, asshole. Can you decipher that?

Olivia's eyes are shooting daggers at the alien form. She notices him squint slightly at her retort, but never blink all the way. He doesn't appear to have eyebrows or eyelashes. When she tries to speak again verbally, her words are immediately snatched away. However, she can still hear the sounds of the craft as it goes through a series of some kind of systems check.

The only way to communicate with me is by using your mind. I understand why you are upset but after you experience what we have planned we will wipe your memories clean. You'll return to your rocket none the worse for wear.

Mithra advances until he is just inches from Olivia's livid face. She feels incredibly helpless. Her arms and legs start to feel very heavy. The sensation creeps up to her midsection and neck. She tries to turn away from him but realizes her head is now completely immobile, along with the rest of her body. Mithra's luminescent eyes watch her intently.

Mission control will be able to track every move this ship makes. I'm not afraid of you.

Olivia's gaze exudes continued defiance even though her mind is being manipulated. Two small tears form, despite her supreme effort to stay calm. She's never felt so trapped her entire life. The last thing the commander notices before passing out are the snow-filled monitors around her.

When she comes to, it's a struggle to lift her eyelids. Something cool has been placed on her forehead. It feels strangely comforting. When her eyes finally open all the way she slowly turns her head to the right. It's like looking at images displaced in water. A vague recognition for the object of her scrutiny fails to come to full fruition.

The person lying next to me-who is she? Where am I? Who am I?

Olivia feels no fear whatsoever. Turning her head to her left, her vision clears slightly. She can see the outline of another person.

This is strange. I have no idea what my name is or where I am. Yet, I'm as calm as a sleeping cat on a Sunday afternoon. Why are other people here with me and why are we lying on these airborne tables? My head feels slightly heavy. I'm good, though. In fact, I'm so fricking comfortable now. I could lie here forever.

Looking to the right again, the commander realizes her memory is shot. Way back, in the furthest reaches of her mind, where some are known to go when they're on the high of their life while under the influence of various mind-altering journeys, something fires up the notion she knows both of the humans. Olivia's consciousness slips down into a zen-like state. Spider-thin memories hang for a split second for her to grab but rapidly dissolve away like snowflakes melting on pavement. She smiles, as a feeling of immense comfort permeates her neural pathways.

I've never felt so relaxed. Whatever is happening, can happen. Ah, what's this I see?

Chapter Three-Mind Games

Olivia floats back to a more cognizant state of consciousness, inside the hull of a huge spaceship. Ironically, the design of the craft is quite similar to the Pentagon building, possessing five sides, like the iconic government landmark in Washington, DC. Hundreds of interconnecting passages lie within the interior. Its outer surface is covered in a bright gold material which appears to be constantly moving, as if the ship is about to morph to a new location, which it often does. Olivia is surrounded by highly advanced lab equipment flashing indecipherable readings.

Mithra appears next to her suspended table and punches a button on its side with something akin to a human finger. The action produces a round hologram containing her complete medical history which he reads quickly. It vanishes into thin air like a coin in a magician's hand. Mithra nods slowly. He gazes down at the commander's serene face for a few seconds. She holds his gaze; the fear and anger she felt before is gone, replaced with nothing more than slight curiosity.

Prominent eyes on the Reji's face are as black as an abandoned coal mine cavern. There is no separation of pupil from iris. The nose is small and flat with two vertical slits which dilate periodically, as if the creature is breathing in the air inside the ship, although no inhalation or exhalation can be heard. His slightly transparent torso fades away into indiscernible features of a lower extremity. Mithra floats in close.

Greetings again, earthling. I hope you are less apprehensive now. I have taken great pains to assure you and your fellow crew members are as comfortable as possible. Welcome aboard Mother Rejenitus. The largest solar-driven spacecraft of Reji. We have paused our return trip home to conduct, for lack of a better description, a meeting of the minds. Our home star is a mere 10,000 light years away. Reji craft travel at speeds beyond human comprehension.

Olivia, still slightly groggy from whatever is flowing through her body, returns Mithra's intense gaze with a hint of amusement in her eyes. She clears her throat and asks for a drink of water. Mithra taps the air, as if he has just summoned a waiter to bring the check. A cup of liquid with a straw is brought to Olivia's parched lips. She eagerly drinks the delicious elixir. It succeeds in awakening her senses. Mithra taps the air again and the cup disappears.

I don't feel afraid in the least. In fact, I feel damn good. This a trip all right. I don't care if it lasts forever. Hell, I don't even care what my own name is. No identity. No problem.

Mithra floats away to inspect the other two occupants of the lab, Veronica and Susan, who also lie in a state of happy submission. The vital statistics of all three women continue to be monitored. Olivia hears a low hum in the stillness of the room. She turns her head slowly, as if she's dreaming. Everything is in slow motion. He speaks to her again with his mind.

I'm saving you for last, Olivia. You are welcome to watch what happens, but it might ruin the surprise for you. Just know, the result will be something quite pleasing. Remember, you can only use telepathy to communicate with me.

Mithra's translucent form now hangs over the relaxed body of the female to Olivia's left, who gazes up at the alien with a look that relays she will not object to anything that is being planned, eyebrows raised and a crooked half smile on her lips. Mithra's shape assumes a prone position approximately one foot above the woman. Olivia can't help but be fascinated by what is transpiring. It is difficult to completely squelch a human's curiosity, for the indomitable trait has been driving homo sapiens since the beginning of their existence. Without this characteristic, mankind would still be in the throes of a complacent, childlike intellect, huddling together for warmth against the cold night.

Olivia notices Mithra's head has moved to within inches of the woman's. His eyes are so large they protrude and pulsate. After a brief delay, the female's back arches off the suspended table, arms limply dangling by her sides, fingertips brushing the table's surface. Her body trembles and Olivia can detect a thin stream of moving particles flow from Mithra's groin area into hers. He holds the woman's gaze for several minutes until the particles slow and eventually disappear. The human body jerks suddenly several times before resuming its original position with eyes closed and a blissful smile on her face. Olivia still hears only the sounds of the craft and instrumentation, yet her mesmerized gaze bears witness to the ritual-like scene.

Mithra performs the exact same actions over the other female while Olivia watches. The two humans are then transported out of the lab. The air becomes supercharged as her thoughts formulate increasing excitement.

I'm ready and willing for whatever is coming. If only I could remember who I am and where I'm going. I suppose it's just as well. Here he comes again...

Olivia closes her eyes for a few seconds, her brows knitted as she tries to concentrate on any clues from her past. It's useless. Nothing comes into her head. No memories of her youth or preceding life. When she opens them, she finds herself looking straight into Mithra's jet-black orbs.

Just relax and enjoy this. It will end like nothing you have ever experienced before.

Down, down, down. The walls of the chamber melt away. Olivia has the sensation of falling. It's thrilling, as if she deployed a parachute while skydiving, just in the nick of time. All her senses come alive making the impending buildup palpable. She hears wind rushing past her ears causing the hair on the back of her neck to stand up. A tingling sensation pricks the top of her head and slowly creeps down her shoulders. Bright lights flicker, drawing her enraptured vision into an abyss of photonic pleasure.

My god, this feels like I'm pleasuring myself-but a thousand times better. The thought does not embarrass her at all. She's locked into Mithra's gaze as faint tingling moves in tantalizing increments down to her waist where it pauses momentarily. Mithra's deep voice washes over her willing body. The commander's back arches even more in expectant pleasure, a silent moan escaping her mouth.

Here comes the best part, Olivia. I've saved your climax for last. Feel my presence in your very core. Let it enter you and consume you. That's it. Feel it.

The sensation encircles her hips. Her body shudders as the teasing vibration proceeds down between partially open legs. She widens them excitedly, her thighs quiver in anticipation. The pulsing moves to her sweet spot, driving an intense orgasm that reverses direction back to her endorphin-charged brain. Mild shock currents race through her visual pathways, firing dormant neurons into a supercharged state of lucidity. The meaning of the universe fills her head. Its purpose is made clear, presented in split second, panoramic images which flash before closed eyes. The mental climax lingers, enveloping all her hyper-tuned senses with the aftereffect of mind-boggling knowledge.

Suddenly, it's over. The transfer of alien particles is complete. Olivia, like the other females, collapses back on the suspended surface. Exhaustion takes over. The experience has already begun to creep from her memory like the path of low tide, steadily returning to the protective arms of the ocean it follows. A serene smile plays on her lips and she sleeps peacefully. Mithra watches her intently. His eyes turn an even deeper shade of midnight black. This particular human attracts him over the others. He enjoyed giving her such intense pleasure, both physically and mentally. Perhaps his self-imposed rule of limiting the number of mating sessions with individual life forms to only once will need to be broken. She has stirred something new within his alien mitochondria and it's very enticing.

Chapter Four-Explain Yourself

"Quantum-One. This is Operator 51 in mission control. Do you copy? We have been trying to reach you for two hours."

Olivia opens her eyes. She's back inside the spacecraft with the remaining crew members who sit with befuddled expressions on their faces. They've just come to also. Although system stats reflect a two-hour progression of time, what transpired during this hiatus is anyone's guess. None of the crew have any ideas to explain their loss of memory. All they can do is step back into the present.

There has been no pause in the trajectory toward the red planet. The majority of Q-One's systems are controlled by Earth-based programs. It could likely reach Mars without the assistance of the crew but then what? Human participation in a successful exodus into the cosmos is not just an option. It's a requirement. Humanoids, although used on the colony for various tasks, do not possess reproductive capability. Procreation must be continued. The more people that accomplish this on IVOSS the better.

"Mission control, this is Commander Newman. I copy and apologize." Olivia views Operator 51 on her overhead holomon. "

"This might be hard to believe but we were apparently in some kind of trance. Like Mesmer himself knocked us out. We feel fine now though and completely alert." Olivia looks at each of her crew members to make sure they all flash a thumbs-up.

"Your video feeds of us-what happened during those two hours? What did you observe?" She is still trying to grasp what occurred.

"Commander Newman, that's the thing. We lost all video comms, too. Glad to see your faces. Maybe the craft passed through galactic flare interference which managed to compromise the communication software. We were unable to retrieve any data from within your crew modules during those two hours. Mission control was stumped.

Olivia directs her attention to Nick who is busy double checking past activity reports. He shakes his head unbelievably. The reports match hers. There's an obvious two-hour gap in the time stamps. What the hell. Changing back to current status, she downplays the incident.

"Operator 51, I'm sure there's a logical explanation we will eventually figure out. I think our efforts are best directed toward the mission objective. Any change in ETA?" The pragmatic nature she was born with aids in maintaining composure of her voice tone and facial features. She smiles into the lens.

"No change, commander. Ground control's advising physician suggests at least seven hours of rest in the sleep pods. If you haven't noticed, blood pressure readings on you and your crew during the time loss were markedly elevated. They've returned to near normal now. Listen to some sleep music, relax and regroup when you awaken."

"Roger. We're headed back to the sleep module now. Talk soon."

Inside the module there are no video feeds. Vital stats are non-stop, of course, relayed to mission control via fitness trackers worn on their wrists. Oliva gathers her crew for a brief discussion.

"Dr. Dorfmeyer, I hadn't noticed the spike in our bp numbers until the operator brought it to my attention. What do you make of it?"

"They *are* still slightly elevated. I picked up on it right away after I regained consciousness. Even though we don't know the cause, it doesn't warrant any special concern at this early juncture. A good, long sleep will most likely restore normal readings. Particularly, since none of us have ever had hypertension in the past. In the unlikely event that medication is needed, we have an ample supply. Is anyone feeling faint or suffering from a headache?"

Every crew member shakes their head no. V looks at Susan and smiles.

"Doc, to be honest, I felt really good after waking up from whatever put us out. The sensation is still with me. I'm surprised at the blood pressure numbers. Why would ours be even higher than the men?" She points out the difference.

"Hard to tell." Susan says. "Let's get some shuteye." The doctor sheds gear next to her sleep pod, using titanium clips to attach items on a black strap for quick repossession. Otherwise, they would float all over the ship. I'll manually recheck everyone's bp when we wake up."

Stepping into her pod she gently shuts the door. A voice command starts her favorite relaxation music-soft classical. She leans back on the thickly padded pod wall, shuts her eyes, and allows the questions invading her mind to slowly fade away. Sleep diffuses the last one, eventually replacing it with a sweet, relaxing dream. James and Zoe laugh while they build a sandcastle on a pristine Caribbean beach. Susan sits beside them and they snuggle in close. A soft breeze stirs their sun-lightened curls, catching natural highlights. They smile when they hear mom whisper in their ears that she will love them forever. Frothy, warm tendrils of water creep closer and closer, but in her idyllic dream, the castle remains unchanged, even after gentle waves overtake their spot on the white sand, as if nothing in the world can destroy its design or the special moment in time.

Within his pod, Nick is thinking about Olivia. He wonders what will happen to their relationship when they arrive at IVOSS. Will she be too busy, diving into various research and development projects or will their orders involve working together? His thoughts drift back to when he was in high school. He dated quite a few girls. None of the relationships lasted long. They were temporary diversions from classes and football practice, meant to appease a feverish rise in testosterone. The dates involved quick sex and empty promises on his part, like a revolving door stuck on repeat. He didn't actually have a serious significant other until midway through attending the US Naval Academy. One night, at an off-campus party, he met a striking blonde name Jenna. They started to spend as much time together as possible. After Nick graduated, he proposed and they were married, right before his acceptance into NASA's astronaut pool.

Nick's relationship with his wife was great, until the subject of children came up. Jenna had reluctantly agreed to have a baby after his third lunar mission. She led him to believe that she wanted a family but then sidestepped her way to a gynecological visit and requested Norplant. His ex kept the fact she was back on birth control a secret until the night he found a pharmaceutical handout tossed carelessly in her bathroom wastebasket. She told him her career in marketing was more important. It was the beginning of the end for their marriage. The trust was gone and so were any feelings he had for her. Lost in a whirlpool of depression, Nick made the difficult decision to file for divorce one month before his selection as assistant commander of the Mars mission.

Now is the time to let Olivia know I'm crazy about her. We've worked together for a few years. At times, it seems like she can read me so well. Damn, that woman is fire and I don't want to let her slip away.

He thinks about her long, honey brown hair. She usually wears it pulled back but the few times she's worn it loose have made him appreciate just how gorgeous it is. He imagines her on top of him, soft strands brushing his hard, naked body as he gazes into smoldering, green eyes. Nick becomes aroused. The erection presses into his clothing. He strokes it for a few seconds, sighs, and then forces the image from his head.

Sleep, Nick. Sleep.

Chapter Five-IVOSS Prepares

The Martian sol begins innocently. Recently elected president of IVOSS, Retired Lt. Gen. Griffin Peters, starts his third cup of coffee since arriving inside headquarters at the crack of dawn. Orders from Earth have recently been issued to check and crosscheck everything is in place for the arrival of Quantum One. He punches a button on a wrist Solcam. After a few seconds, the crisp image of his right-hand man, First Lt. Miles Hamilton, appears.

Miles, like the Lt. Gen., wears a standard uniform issued by the colony. Relaxed dress codes favor comfortable attire, enacted to promote good will amongst international countries represented. The acronym IVOSS, embroidered in black, stands out prominently on a light blue shirt, with the "O" colored reddish/brown to represent the beautiful planet citizens seek to colonize. Underneath the lettering is an American flag. As a welcome gift, every incoming person receives two shirts with their native country's flag and their name and title added.

"How are things shaping up at the landing site, Miles? I've been told the window of time for a safe approach has been shortened due to a possible dust storm." Peters fires the question out, then takes a quick gulp of his black coffee, burning his tongue slightly. He glares into the Solcam, swearing under his breath.

"Sir, the arrival crew has been ready for months." Hamilton is ready with a response, lifting his clean-shaven chin with assured confidence.

"They've rehearsed contingency plans in case the landing sequence needs to be altered for a downgrade in conditions. All personnel are operating in high gear."

"The storm doesn't look to be any more than an increase in winds, according to our lead meteorologist. I've also ordered additional stabilizing measures for the airbridge to get the crew inside safely. Two mobile rocket hangers have been positioned to afford spacecraft protection. If one gets damaged, we will utilize the backup. No stones have been left unturned, sir."

"Excellent. I will see you in the morning." Peters ends the video call, then pushes an ergonomic rolling chair a few feet back from the hydraulic desk so he can stand. Although average in height, he has maintained a powerful physique from daily workouts. A quiet strength is his greatest asset. Striding to the shatterproof window, he gazes solemnly at the red, Martian dirt, vivid blues eyes scanning the horizon. Small dust devils blow up from the regolith, rising like camouflaged lizards from the planetary surface. Griffin's gaze is held on the panorama. It's currently summertime, when dust storms are the most prevalent. He hopes Hamilton is right about being prepared.

Christ, this is the last fucking thing I need during my inaugural week. It better go smoothly, or I'll be facing hell from back home. I guess it wouldn't be the first time...

Griffin heads out the door to meet with top members of his fledgling administration.

IVOSS has grown by leaps and bounds since its initial construction near the Tharsis region, an area full of huge caves, some of which have been sealed and pressurized to form passageways for the colony, connecting natural formations to those erected by hand. Lava tubes are accessible for an ample ice source which is converted to water.

There have been numerous presidents prior to Peters. Not all have been officers of the military. Each is limited to a 2-year term. International countries represented on the colony supply two voting delegates in election years. An officer and non-enlisted citizen cast their votes, assuring the helm is taken over by a fresh mind. Impeachment proceedings can and will proceed in the event of flagrant behavior.

Russian past president, Dr. Aleksander Balabanov, just completed his term. After serving honorably, he is returning to the medical facilities and will oversee health maintenance of the colony's citizens. He manages a team of health care providers. Dr. Susan Dorfmeyer's arrival is something he is looking forward to. She will be co-managing patients with him. Her extensive research on reproductive studies is sure to provide the most up-to-date information and assistance to those wishing to procreate and remain on Mars. The more young minds for the future, the better.

Inside a high-tech laboratory, Dr. Balabanov continues to gather data on each Mars citizen, from birth to the present. Every person who chooses to remain on the red planet, must receive in-depth physical examinations, every six months. Public reports provide updates, although exact names are never released. Health summaries reveal the top ailments contracted during the prior reporting period, along with recovery success percentages. Incidents of serious infection have remained low throughout the years.

IVOSS's current population stands at five thousand people. All children have been born on Mars. They represent approximately 20% of the total and the future of the colony's survival. Their knowledge of Earth is limited, of course, having never experienced first-hand its extreme beauty or been part of the planet's volatile history. Although the village has a large library with thousands of books available, most kids depend on their parents or mentors to fill them in. Education is provided by accessing online tutorials or group classes.

As the day progresses, First Lt. Hamilton watches a holcast from lead meteorologist Ryan Forrester. He states the impending storm, if it even occurs, will only produce mild winds and minimal surface soil movement, according to recent weather modules. No landing diversion should be needed. Hamilton breathes a sigh of relief and heads to the assembly hall. A Q-One welcome committee will be selected at tonight's weekly public meeting.

First Flight Assembly Hall is gargantuan, having been designed to hold forty thousand people. It will be a long time before it reaches capacity limit. On the ground level of the structure, at dead center, is a massive stage that rotates. Speakers and lighting hang far above it. Several jumbotrons allow closer viewing of whomever is in the spotlight.

Media relations manager Dawn Hiatt watches people pour into the doorways. They proceed down to the closest seats; their voices remind her of some of the concerts she used to enjoy on Earth during her college years. There's excitement in the audience over Quantum One's arrival. It means new faces along with a host of assignments to accomplish. Dawn and two assistants sit at a rectangular table on stage. Microphones are attached to their blue shirts. A metal box containing the names of citizens who have offered to form the welcome committee is in front of them. Dawn opens the meeting at 7 o'clock sharp.

"Good evening!" Dawn rises from her seated position. "I hope this last week has been productive for you. I want to thank all who chose to attend, especially everyone whose names are in the pool for possible selection. Let's give them a round of applause, please!"

Loud clapping echoes in the vastness of the gargantuan hall. Dawn smiles and waits for it to subside.

"Are there any questions or concerns before I draw the committee appointees? Seeing no raised hands, she proceeds to draw the names of five individuals. The selected people rise to another round of applause as their names are called out and take a seat at the table with the other assistants.

A brief movie about proper procedures plays on the trons, reminding attendees that newcomers receive the best accommodations, etc, etc . The aim is to get them to stay on Mars permanently. Suggestions are made for the welcome celebration, which usually takes place a couple of days after the crew's arrival. It's a challenge, because many wish to return to something or someone on Earth.

An increasing number of people back home anxiously await the opportunity to join in the exodus; commercially produced rockets are utilized for the private sector. Thus far, Mars' populace is mainly made up of scientists, doctors, and NASA employees. Each left their former lives on Earth behind to be part of something much bigger than themselves. The challenges of space exploration pull mankind like a magnet pulls metal shavings. Is there risk? Of course. Since when has that stopped us?

Chapter Six-T-Minus One Hour

Quantum One sounds like it's breathing softly. Systems engineer Devon McDonald cocks his head while punching commands on an eye-level holomon. His ears are constantly hyper tuned to the various noises made by the massive rocket as it steadily locks into its landing target. He could swear the "whooshes" have become more frequent, as if the craft itself is excited for the imminent final approach and needs additional air to calm itself.

Landing Pad Five, Skyport Sector 2A, is in direct sight. Although the planet's atmosphere is too thin to produce lightning strikes like those seen on Earth, dust storms are capable of strong electrical discharge activity. It necessitates the construction of towering lightning rods around the pad. Their red beacons blink off and on, similar to a lighthouse's pulsing signal, warning incoming ships about dangerous shorelines.

Devon thinks about the talented minds at NASA he was honored to collaborate with. They worked as a team, designing and perfecting software programs which maintain autonomous function of spaceships. However, he's been given on board override capability, as have Nick and Olivia, just in case something funky happens, albeit this high-level clearance has a limited time window for enactment.

McDonald, a sci-fi movie junkie, thinks about HAL, the onboard computer who Dave battles in Arthur C. Clarke's classic film adaptation, 2001 A Space Odyssey. AI is wonderful for the most part, but can software-driven programs or androids ever be trusted entirely? They are not always failsafe, even in the most ideal conditions. Throw a wrench in and the result can be catastrophic. It's Murphy's Law. One must be prepared for it.

The parachute implementation sequence begins. By the time the primary and backup chutes deploy fully, Q-One's crew capsule will be quite close to the Mars surface. Pad Five sits a safe fifty miles from the largest drill site on the planet. Here, ice chunks long buried in deep caverns, are mined like expensive diamonds for conversion to water and rocket fuel. Mining is paused when rocket landings take place as a safeguard.

"Well, crew, this it. Everyone, please return to your seats for the final approach and separation." Olivia's words reflect the excitement felt by everyone. "Devon, are we on track for an arrival time close to 10:00 LST?"

"Yes, Commander, give or take a few minutes either way." Devon cracks a smile at the rather vague confirmation and Olivia smiles back. She loves how he isn't afraid to pull her chain a little. McDonald was first in his class at MIT and the highest scorer in system design and testing amongst thousands of applicants who were competing for the mission.

Sustained accuracy is sometimes impossible in space, due to revised mathematical formulas or yet unknown factors affecting outcome. There is simply no way to predict everything, when scientific information is constantly changing. Spontaneity is just as important as intellect. You must be a fast thinker. Devon possesses both assets. In fact, the commanders and other crew members plan on nominating him to run in the next IVOSS presidential election. If victorious, he will be the first black man to oversee the colony since its inception. His crewmates know he possesses all the necessary traits to be a great leader.

The red planet awaits them, its myriad of colors changing periodically. As they prepare for capsule separation, each astronaut wonders what kind of mark they will make on the human timeline of planetary colonization. Look at how far things have progressed since 1965, when NASA's Mariner, the very first spacecraft to reach the Mars surface, landed successfully. No one expected the rapid progression of development. The pioneers on IVOSS have adapted to the Martian environment far beyond anyone's expectations, following the huge success of NASA's Gateway and thriving lunar outposts.

On the red planet, construction is booming between several dormant volcano tops. A great deal of lava beneath the surface of Mars remained in subterranean locations during massive volcanic eruptions, creating huge rock formations instead. Researchers have recently revealed evidence of amino acids near locations where ocean and lake water once flowed freely on the Martian terrain, still surviving in incredibly deep drill sites. Where else could the building blocks of life be hiding?

"Quantum One-capsule separation initiated. Stand by."

"Copy that," Olivia responds. "Q-One capsule separation initiated." Much sharper details of the surface come into view through the craft's round windows, located laterally. The capsule landing zone is one mile from Pad Five.

Veronica has never been so pumped inside. She's been waiting for this opportunity a long time.

I am going to soak in every goddamn detail of this mission. I bet mom is glued to NASA live coverage right now. She loves this shit as much as I do.

"Capsule separation complete, Commander. Parachute one at one hundred percent deployment. Backup parachute at ninety percent"

The crew responds with cheers, looking out the windows and chattering excitedly. Their adrenaline is high.

Quantum One, having released its precious human cargo, slowly turns around, beginning supersonic retropropulsion, the final stage before contact with the launch/landing pad.

The capsule, now at a safe distance from the rocket, will utilize three layered heat shields, providing protection from the lethal Mars atmosphere. Q-Ones' crew switches to holmons instead of views from the windows.

"Is that storm debris I see rotating over the landing zone?" It wasn't there a minute ago! Shit!" Nick has his crew comm channel on so everyone can weigh in. The pad is becoming increasingly difficult to make out. "What the hell?"

"Devon, we probably should have overridden the approach command. What do you think?" Olivia was so caught up in the overall view of the planet she didn't notice the rapidly worsening conditions. Now, the window of time to abort has expired.

"Blame me, Commander. I was relying on prior weather data predictions saying the storm would be mild. Apparently, mission control was, too."

"Commander Newman, this is Operator 67. We're receiving image and updated storm tracking data of a pop-up dust storm. Rapidly declining conditions have unexpectedly occurred within the last few minutes. Unfortunately, final descent of Q-One cannot be aborted, as you know. The crew capsule landing is on track to transpire without a hitch."

"Roger," Olivia replies calmly. "I hope the pads homing sensors are still able to guide it in. Our feeds are full of whirling, crimson regolith." Olivia looks at Nick before talking to the remaining crew members on the shared, private line. Their eyes lock momentarily.

"Well, guys, looks like Q-One will come in hot and blind." They respond with nervous laughter. "At least we're safe in here. Check out the huge shock pad to cushion our impact! Damn, the airbridge has sustained damage. We'll need to disembark via a rover.

"An entire section is gone!" Susan exclaims. "Looks like this storm is going to be bad."

Ret. Lt. General Peters and Ft. Lt. Hamilton watch from the large windows of pad hanger one's ground level. Crew members scurry around frantically. Peters face contorts in disgust.

"Looks like the weather forecast was wrong." He wants this event to go off perfectly, seeing as it's the first incoming arrival under his command. Now, the realization that something serious could happen has dampened his mood and the day.

This rocket is carrying crucial equipment for the colony. Damn dust storms to hell.

"Hamilton, is there anything that can be done?" Peters starts to pace back and forth. "Q-One needs to touchdown within the programmed landing window. Where is the lead meteorologist?"

"Right here, sir." Weatherman Forrester joins the group. When he sees the scowling face of Lt. Gen. Peters, he's quick to absolve himself of any blame.

"A pop-up storm of this size is extremely rare. Keep in mind the strongest winds should not exceed 60 miles per hour. The landing is at only a slightly increased risk of developing problems.

"I hope you are right. Hamilton, are the ground crew and medical teams ready?" Peters moves closer to the window, watching the rocket's descent.

Hamilton is starting to worry but hides it well, as usual. He and Forrester approach, observing a ground crew unaccustomed to this kind of event.

"Yes, sir. I've ordered additional personnel. It looks hectic out there, but the crews will handle it."

Skyport 5 is in high alert mode. Thus far, the winds of the dust storm have stayed below fifty miles per hour, but during the last few minutes, they have increased to gusts over seventy miles per hour. Storms this strong rarely occur in the Tharsis region. The timing is horrible.

Chapter Seven-Shake, Rattle & Roar

NASA's most advanced rocket points straight up from the Mars terrain, as if the hand of Thor is manipulating a toy model. Changed from the horizontal position it formerly held, its final landing approach is in progress. The crew capsule, having completed nominal separation, approaches IVOSS' massive shock pad, one mile away.

It's not going to be so simple for Quantum One. A pop-up dust storm is gaining wind speed, blowing sand and debris around Pad Five. Sludge buildup seeps into electronic sensor casings on two of the four landing arms, resulting in only partial support of the huge rocket as it lurches onto the pad. Simultaneously, a strong wind gust hits, causing it to heave from precarious mooring after initial contact.

Q-One's crew celebrates a perfect landing on the pad with high fives and a few "fuck yeahs!", then pauses to watch video feeds from inside their small capsule. Nothing like this has ever happened. They see the massive rocket leaning sharply to its port side. Commander Newman cringes in spite of herself.

What the hell happened to accurate weather forecasts? Can't we protect our incoming rockets better than this? Jesus.

"That she-beast is in trouble. The storm must be damn serious if it's wreaking havoc on deployment mechanisms." Devon grimly points out the obvious. "They grossly underestimated the storm's strength. If those arms don't begin to function as intended, the entire rocket is in danger of toppling over. Shit, our feed is awful. It's killing me that I can't help." Devon looks down dejectedly. Veronica tries to make him feel better.

"This is not your fault, Devon. Look, something's happening." Her kind eyes direct the engineer's back to the unfolding scene.

It will take too long for the mobile hangers to move toward the listing rocket. It needs to be manually realigned immediately. Inside hanger one, an emergency intervention team has been formed, wearing gleaming white terrasuits topped by grey helmets. The massive door rises like the jaws of a python opening to encompass its prey. Just inside the building, two super extension ladders with wheels are rolled onto the automated runway strip. The workers divide, so that one half is grouped with each ladder. Tethered to one another at the waist by elasticized belts, they start the moving runway to reach the landing pad.

Gale force winds continue to increase. Views from space show the system has almost completely enveloped the southern hemisphere. Originally thought to be only a brief atmospheric disturbance with moderate winds, the storm has morphed into a record-setting event. Gusts are now being recorded up to ninety mph. Baby dust devils have become towering whirlwinds of debris, some reaching extremely high altitudes. Dr. Dorfmeyer, a religious woman, says a little prayer to herself, wishing again that her crucifix could be touched for comfort.

We need those lab supplies and medications to care for colonists. Please God, get the rocket stabilized.

It's a good thing the pad ladders are super weighted to withstand such an event. Even with lighted helmets and illumination of the pad itself, it's extremely difficult to see through the vortex of red dust. An AI voice, which usually reverberates from numerous intercoms, becomes muffled in the thickened air.

WARNING. ROCKET PO..si...tion Cri...ti...cal..... The computer-generated message slows and stutters as ferocious winds suck monotone words into a tunnel where eventually they die out. After a brief respite, it drones again. A Skyport crisis is underway.

The auto runway encircles the entire pad. It comes to a stop on the left side of the rocket. Holding tight to their weighted ladder, half the crew roll it off next to the faulty arm pad. The circular strip begins to rotate again, moving the remaining ladder and manpower to the other side. Ladder team one climbs the extension to the arm mechanism height, fighting the buffeting winds.

Teflon umbrellas with long side flaps unfold to shield their platform workspace, luckily deploying as ordered. Attached via ultra-thin cables to terrasuits, small brushes and cans of pressurized air are utilized to clean the electronic sensors which control arm function. The same is done to the opposite compromised arm. Protective coverings, formerly viewed as not necessary, are put in place.

One of the workers stops to gaze through a clear patch of the umbrella. All he can see is Martian muck. The surface of the planet cannot be discerned at all. It reminds him of a self-awareness retreat he went to fifteen years ago. The night some kick-ass shatter lived up to its name, shattering his senses into a similar mind fuck, as if The Rolling Stones were singing about him. He grunts and turns back to the task at hand.

It takes several minutes before the green sensor lights kick on, followed by jointed landing arms extending to their proper positions. Additional support cables are pulled from the pad so the ground crew can attach them to any of the hundreds of grommets located on the outer surface of the craft. The whine of pulleys is heard as Quantum One gets positioned back into its correct, completely upright position, her massive weight being cradled like a child of the universe.

The storm continues to batter the workers as they climb down from the ladders and step onto the now stationary runway. It also decides to malfunction, leaving them no choice but to walk back to the hanger. High winds deter their return trip, almost sucking them into a blowing abyss. Pellets bounce off their helmets like small shards of glass pinging a window. The handrails they hold onto are lifesavers.

Finally, safety is reached inside the hanger. The overhead door comes down with seal-smacking assurance. Now that the rocket is steady, a secondary team commands the mobile backup hanger to move into protective positioning. Luckily, it makes it in the violent storm.

"Jesus. Did anyone expect the weather to get this bad today?" A woman from the first group laughs nervously, adjusting her helmet attachments. "That was way too close for me." She fingers the pellet marks on her terrasuit.

"You're not kidding, Janice. We're good to extract Quantum One's crew now," says a muscular guy standing next to her. He punches a button on his wrist device which summons a large, enclosed rover, designed to hold up to twenty people. His extraction team, consisting of four people, climbs in. The hanger door creeks up again, as if the cast of Cats waits behind it. If only this trip could be as entertaining as the famed Broadway musical.

They begin a laborious trek toward the capsule shock pad. It's slow going. Large debris chunks batter the outside of the vehicle as it slowly but steadily approaches.

"Let's stay on our toes, team," the big guy reminds the others. He must be in charge. Janice looks over her shoulder as the hanger door descends. It fills her with a sense of dread.

Chapter Eight-There She Blows

"How the hell did this damn storm grow so quickly?" Veronica knows her crewmates don't know the answer any more than she does. It rattles her pragmatic chain. A static-infused comm fills the capsule as if on cue to provide an update.

"Quantum One. Welcome to Mars! This is Mike from the Skyport Transfer Team. Sorry about the unexpected storm severity. We are in position to commence crew transfer to a rover. The vehicle will withstand winds up to 80 mph. We've already had wind gusts approaching that, so the extraction needs to be quick. Advise tethering together. It's just a couple of steps to onboard but let's avoid any risk of separation."

Inside the capsule, Q-One's crew is already thinking the same thing. They're clipped to one another. Olivia, as commander, will be first to exit, followed by Nick, Veronica, Devon, and Susan. The newness of their surroundings and the ongoing storm has their adrenaline going. However, they've trained for scenarios like this. Any unease is tempered by a determined readiness to adapt as a team.

Adaptation—how all species evolve. Like a seahorse changing the color of its skin, utilizing camouflage against predators, homo sapiens also change or mutate. These mutations can occur via outside or internal influence. Within the cells and molecules of matter that provide a basis of life, adapting DNA can be susceptible to all types of manipulation. By things found on planet Earth, or beyond. Mars is set to become a location in The Milky Way Galaxy where new biological classifications come into existence.

Olivia catches Nick's eye and smiles. She wonders what he's thinking behind those hazel eyes of his. It's so easy to get lost in them.

"Roger Mike, we're clipped together and will begin the hatch opening sequence." Olivia motions for Devon to voice the command. After a few seconds, a loud hiss fills the capsule as the seal breaks. The door slowly lowers, becoming a walking plank that will be traversed to the waiting rover, less than twenty feet away. Q-One's crew is greeted by a blowing mess. They are unable to see any distinct features of the Martian terrain as they step onto the inverted hatch segment.

Gale force winds continue to grow in intensity, filling the astronaut's helmets with a muffled roar. Although it's a short distance to travel, they are forced to lean into the storm's vicious onslaught, which changes direction. It now drives directly against their surging bodies. The resistance is incredible.

After Susan exits, the hatch door immediately shuts. Unfortunately, a good deal of Martian regolith has blown into it. Devon had the foresight to pre-program an automatic vacuum. It senses foreign material, utilizing a snakelike hose which gently sucks the soil into a waste receptable.

Safely aboard the rover, Q-One's crew remove their helmets. Hugs, handshakes and relieved laughter help settle everyone's nerves. It's short-lived however, as within a couple minutes the rover's MMRTG engine begins to cough and sputter.

"Goddamn this piece of shit." Mike likes to cuss. No one cares.

The vehicle lurches twice, throwing the occupants forward. Susan grabs a stationary belt which encircles the inside panels. As it rolls to an agonizing stop, the vehicle shudders with a final, ominous sound.

"Skyport, requesting system assessment asap." Mike orders the remote inspection immediately. "We've stalled out."

"Rover team, stand by. Running diagnostics." The muted reply is static filled. Storm interference is making communication increasingly difficult.

Mike looks at his ground team and shakes his head in disgust before apologizing to the incoming crew.

"This mother just went through a complete test run yesterday with flying colors. I'm not sure what's wrong."

A red-haired guy sitting next to Veronica is quick to speak up.

"Mike, I've worked on these models quite a bit. It's usually a faulty element that causes a breakdown. Or a sensor meltdown. My guess is the element."

Veronica looks at the name on his suit. She sticks out her hand to introduce herself.

"Hi Everett. I'm Veronica. You can call me V. I think you're right. One of the last training sessions I took part in was on radioisotope powered vehicles.

There should be a backup with all the necessary tools to complete a switch in the bin at the rear of the rover."

"That's good to know." Susan laughs nervously. Wind speed has somehow picked up even more. The vehicle has one window on each side. Visibility is still next to zero, other than blowing debris that pummels them incessantly, making it hard to hear each other.

"We should get a diagnostic report in the next few minutes." Mike turns to the blonde girl, raising his voice above the storm outside.

"Janice, how many rovers were available in the hanger when we left?"

The blonde looks at her wrist device for a quick confirmation before answering.

"Five were in ready mode. Three under repair. They can just send another one out to pick-"

A huge gust rocks the rover to the right heavily, sending people sliding on their seats into one another. The wind whipping around them sounds like a fire drill ringing in an elementary school, sending kids out of class and into the hallway for shelter.

"Whoa!" Devon puts his left arm on a steering console for support, taking some weight off his right side which is jammed up against Veronica. He doesn't mind it. She smells good. Damn good. He reminds himself his fiancé, Nicole, is back home, supposedly making wedding plans.

If she's even doing that. I have my doubts.

He can't help but smile at Veronica. It's not like this was his fault. The mission specialist sure doesn't seem to be upset about the unexpected contact.

She seems to like this. He doesn't fail to notice.

The rover creaks before finally rocking back to a more level position, but every few seconds another wind gust threatens to topple it over.

I'd better nip thoughts like that in the bud. Veronica is a good friend of mine with an amazing head on her shoulders. Jesus, I never expected to feel flutters in my pants being so close to her.

"Ground crew. This is hanger support. Element 6FZ7 has been compromised. You can either attempt the repair yourselves or we can send a replacement rover. We've just received confirmation that wind speeds have reached gusts of 90 mph. A new record, unfortunately. Radar reports the storm's area is actually increasing in size. There's no guarantee that a replacement rover can make it to you."

"I can have a new element in within five minutes." Veronica immediately volunteers to complete the dangerous repair. "I just need someone to help me access the casing."

"No problem." Everett grins at her. "Looks like we're the lucky ones with the most experience. I've got you."

Olivia looks at Nick for his opinion.

"I'd hate for another rover to sustain damage in this shit storm. If V and Everett tie off securely, I think they can get the job done, working together. The challenge will be visibility, if they don't get blown across the fricking terrain first!"

"The supply bin has a cover that will completely encase V so she can see to perform the repair. It's magnetized for attachment to the vehicle." Everett slides the bin panel open and smiles. "Score! And here's the replacement element. Easy peasy folks."

Mike knows that Everett is his top maintenance tech and after learning that Veronica recently trained on a rover exactly like this one places his mindset in agreement with Nick's.

"Okay, you two. Be sure to tie off first thing."

"Hanger control. Our team will be replacing the element as soon as we can. Hold release of another rover. The winds are really whipping us around."

Veronica remains seated, taking a rope from Everett. She quickly wraps it around her waist twice before passing it back so he can do the same. The end of the rope has heavy-duty clips which slap against his thigh. V nods at Olivia with a determined look in her eyes. She's been waiting for an opportunity to show her team that she's not afraid of dangerous situations. When things get difficult, she's always found a way through sheer determination.

The two volunteers stand and move toward the back of the rover. It's hard to keep their balance. Clutching overhead straps helps them get to the door.

V has tools and the replacement element in a bag attached to her waist. Everett doublechecks the tarp is tied to his wrist, so it won't blow away. He will deploy it before the repair is begun.

"Okay, Mike." Veronica gives some last-minute instructions. "When the door opens, make sure all of you are holding onto your straps so you don't get sucked out into oblivion. The first thing I'm going to do is attach to the outside rail. Everett will, too. Luckily, the element casing is located within a couple feet of the exit.

"You got it." Mike says. "Keep your comms open. Get out there, stay focused on the task, and replace the mother fucker. Good luck."

Everett stands right behind V as the rover door slides open.

"Let's go!" She shouts, but her words are lost in the vortex.

Chapter Nine-Behold What is Gold

"Everett!" V can barely make out the element's access panel a few feet to the left. "Attach the cover over me as soon as I'm in position!" Her hollow words reverberate in the maintenance tech's helmet.

"Will do!" he shouts loudly, trying to sound confident, although his inner voice belies what comes out of his mouth.

Hope I don't fuck anything up. This storm is damn serious.

Everett unfolds the cover in stages, starting at the top. It's only large enough to protect one person. The wind threatens to snatch it out of his hands, but he holds tight, remembering the last corner is tied to his wrist. Strong peripheral magnets snap onto the outside of the rover. Finally, V is completely enclosed. She feels like a construction worker outside a skyscraper, standing on a scaffold that has been blown into a huge pane of vibrating glass.

"How's it going out there?" Mike stands with his ear pressed to the inner door. All he can hear is the high-pitched whine of the wind. The others listen to the comm, peering as best they can out small windows. "I don't like how long this is taking one goddamned minute."

Wish I was home making breakfast for James and Zoe right now. Susan is starting to wonder if this mission will be worth it. *Stop being so pessimistic, doc. We'll be safely transferred in no time.*

"I've gained access to the unit, Mike. The hard part is keeping my body stationary so I can manipulate these tools. Good thing they're magnetic, too. Everett is on me like white on rice." V laughs in an attempt to downplay the danger. She's thankful for the extra weight on her backside.

Everett blushes a crimson red that almost matches the color of his short, curly hair. He's relieved the flush is unseen. Although more exposed to the elements than V, he's managing to stay somewhat stationary by grabbing one of the rover's guardrails.

Suddenly, out of the corner of his eye, a gold streak flashes by. It's so brief he thinks he imagined it. There it is again, overhead now! Shards of blindingly bright, golden light exploding behind him.

Is this some kind of joke? Why the increasing pressure in my helmet? The tech blinks, pale blue eyes reflecting a mixture of surprise and growing anxiety.

"Mike, can you see anything happening behind us? I'm observing occasional flashes of —what the hell is that?" Everett's choirboy voice rises as his head turns to see an enormous spacecraft which has replaced towering dirt whirlwinds with something unfathomable.

"What is it?" V's voice, dimmer now. Slowing down, garbled, faint.

My eyes—can't see anything. Why can't I talk. Jesus, please help me....

"I've replaced the element, Mike. Panel closure is all that's left. There's a really bright glow coming through the cover. It must be practically on top of us. Almost done..."

"Get your asses back in here!" Mike and the others are gawking out the window. What they see stops their hearts. A craft so incredibly huge that only a fraction of its massive size can be observed. It shimmers, radiating energy and warmth, dispelling dust storms in its wake. It has no windows or rocket boosters. Exceedingly brilliant, golden sides scintillate in the thin Martian atmosphere creating a mirage-like effect. No humans have ever witnessed anything that resembles this ship. Well, maybe in a movie, but that doesn't count. Hell, this is REAL.

"Everett, take the cover off. I'm done! What's going on out there?" Veronica shouts at the top of her lungs. Shifting her body weight. she realizes his movements mimic hers. The wind has died down, it's eerily quiet.

No answer.

Uh oh. V forces herself to remain calm. *Stay cool.*

"Everett-are you all right?"

Silence. Veronica's skin breaks out in cold goosebumps. Everett's suit may have been breached. His limp body presses against her back. Slowly, she reaches overhead and breaks the magnetic connection of the cover, turning to see what's going on. A dumbfounded gaze takes over her countenance, although her heartrate doubles at the sight of the gargantuan vessel.

A spaceship? Are you fucking kidding me? Here? Why?

She waits until the helmet's photochromatic visor darkens, lessening the bright light that burns her retinas. Finally, she can see through the tech's helmet visor.

Dios Mio. "Everett?" Nothing.

His eyes are closed. He is unresponsive, chin slumped. A thin stream of drool runs down a double chin.

Mike's expletives vaguely register in V's ears.

"Everett. Do you copy? I'm moving back toward the door." Warm breath fogs up the inside of her own visor as she waits for a reply. A pit forms in her stomach. All her senses are hyper tuned.

Maybe he just fainted from the shock of whatever this thing is.

"Mike. Something's happened to Everett. He passed out." Veronica grunts and moves back toward the door, still plastered against the rover, hauling the added burden of Everett. She can feel slight waves of energy being emitted from the craft, like she's a specimen under an electron microscope. She inches her way back.

I can't take my eyes off it... Feeling the door handle. Cold. Inert. Like the person stuck to her.

"Okay, open the door!"

V plunges into the rover along with Everett. Mike and Devon catch the technician's motionless body, gently helping it to the floor. Just before the hatch door closes, a loud swoosh is heard as the megaship dashes up and out of sight, lifting itself with incredible speed. It leaves no trace of having been there. The crew look at each other, stupefied. Shock. Incredible shock at what they've witnessed. A first encounter with...an alien force.

They realize Everett hasn't come around. Arms, ramrod straight, pressed against his torso.

"His vitals are plummeting." Susan rushes to Everett's supine body.

She gently removes the helmet with one hand, supporting his head with the other. Almost immediately, Everett coughs violently. His eyelids flutter as he gasps for air. Small trickles of blood drip from a capillary-laced nose and out crimson ears. Petechial spots erupt on his face and neck. As he loses consciousness, one last agonizing breath gets cut off in mid effort. Susan checks for a pulse, shaking her head when nothing is detected, moving in to check for respirations. None.

"Oh my god-he's hemorrhaging!" Janice's voice reflects the horror that everyone feels. Her face contorts with emotion, a red flush creeping up her neck like a turtleneck shirt gone wild. "What the hell happened to him?"

"Calm down, Janice," Mike orders sternly. "Take a chill pill, for Christ's sake. We need everyone to stay focused."

Susan yells for the portable AED machine. Mike pulls it off the hook and kneels next to her. Life-saving efforts commence. Olivia and Nick join them in the classic four-man team. Finally, after repeated resuscitation attempts, they realize Everett is lost. This shy, barely-out-of-college, carrot-topped man, had no idea what hit him. There aren't any visible signs of suit or helmet malfunction.

"It's got something to do with that goddamn spaceship." Veronica's voice is matter of fact. She cranks her head toward the window. "Look outside-the storm has finally passed over. But that—thing—whatever it was..." V pauses, looking around at the others. She is more pissed off than scared. Dr. Dorfmeyer looks like she just saw a ghost. The others don't appear much better.

Mike punches a button on the console to start the rover.

"Hanger control, we're coming in. Repair completed but we've lost a technician. Stand by for a complete report."

Everyone is quiet during the return trip to the hanger. Everett's dead body lies on the floor of the rover, covered, ironically, with the same tarp he used to shield Veronica's.

Peters and Hamilton wait for them just inside the building. Mike grimly fills them in on what happened, as medics remove Everett's body from the rover.

The acting president stands next to Hamilton with arms crossed, mouth in a straight line. A throbbing pulse can be seen on his neck when he speaks up.

"No alien craft was detected on **our** radars. Are you *sure* it was a ship?" Peters voice is still quietly commanding.

"I saw it right behind me, shortly after Everett passed out. His fatality must be connected to its arrival." Veronica replies impatiently.

Wonder why I wasn't attacked, too. Horrible guilt sets in.

"All the rover occupants observed the ship from the inside." Mike backs up V's adamant claim that the craft was in no way imagined.

Olivia and Nick stare at each other. This mission looks to be laden with fuckery. What's next?

Chapter Ten-Why?

It's the morning after Q-One's precarious landing. Olivia didn't sleep well. Every once in a while, when her mind is troubled, she frequents unpleasant places in her dreams. Places where she is the opposite of the strong persona she portrays on the outer surface. It's hard to be positive and confident one hundred percent of the time. When those memories invade her thoughts, the past creeps in, like a robber sneaking past a dozing security guard.

When she was eleven years old, Olivia attended her little brother Shiloh's soccer match. Midway through, the players and fans saw him collapse on the field. After being revived, he complained of an awful headache. Their parents immediately scheduled an extensive workup, including a CT scan, MRI, and lab work. The neurologist relayed the dire news that her nine-year-old sibling had an inoperable, malignant brain tumor. The family dynamics took a nosedive at the news, understandably.

Olivia was beyond devastated. Shiloh, silly, hyper, and the bravest kid she knew, had only six months to live. She cried in the arms of her parents and then cried herself to sleep the night they told her. The two had been inseparable from the day she saw his little toes and bright, inquisitive brown eyes staring back at her. Those eyes were destined to lose their shine, like an imploding star snuffed out in darkness. It absolutely killed her inside, but she fought to keep a positive attitude around him.

They hung together after school, shooting hoops or riding bikes with neighborhood friends. Summers were so much fun. Remember, if you will, the never-ending days when you were a kid. Sunup to sundown. Countless hours of memories being made. Warm sunshine kissing your skin and the smell of the season all around. Flowers, pine trees, the rich earth beneath bare feet.

Not a care in the world, like it should be for children. Days filled with simple things, like walking in the woods hunting for emerald-green frogs, dozing under moss-coated rocks. Or dropping a line in the small, serene pond a short walk from their two-story house. The best night crawlers could be found after a soaking rain, all over their cracked driveway, slimy bodies crawling and squirming to escape small hands. Fair game for the taking and transfer to styrofoam, dirt-filled containers. Sometimes, the worm stashes went bad in the refrigerator and mom would get irritated. Most were used before that happened.

One day, two months before her brother left his pain-filled days behind, the siblings were seated outside Mercy Hospital on a wooden bench, faces turned up to the early afternoon sun. The warm rays felt so good, coating the backs of their eyelids in an amber glow.

"Livy, do you think rockets will ever be able to fly into the sun?" The question didn't surprise Olivia, because Shiloh loved anything to do with space travel. He had already won several STEM rocket building contests in school. "I mean, what would it be like if we could?" Shi's brown eyes were full of curiosity. Cancer would never take that away.

"I don't see why not, but humans will need to figure out how without getting fried first." Olivia laughed at the time, because, as usual, her little brother asked thought-provoking questions for his age. She hid the fact that the question broke her heart. He put his thin arms around her and planted a weak kiss on her cheek.

"Well, I'm going to help design a rocket that can!" His flushed face was somehow still full of determination. What a courageous kid.

After Shiloh passed, Olivia relied on the love and support of her parents even more. They lost their desire to have another child the day Shi lost his battle with cancer, three days before he would have turned ten.

Her family did the best they could without him. Olivia lived at home until the day she was accepted into the US Naval Academy. The valedictorian title and perfect SAT-ACT scores did not go unnoticed. She was one of less than ten percent of applicants to be accepted. Indiana's rolling, southern hills cradled her parents, as they learned to cope with being empty nesters. Seeing their daughter do so well was worth the tradeoff. They were able to visit her often, along with their son's rocket-etched grave, located in the tree-filled family cemetery a mile away.

I need to get to work. Watch out for me, little bro. Olivia tucks the memories away and faces the new day, heading to the shower.

Dr. Dorfmeyer sits in her dorm, recording a short video.

"Hello family! Quantum One made it, as you already know." Susan tries to appear super pumped.

"I'm still in shock over being on Mars! Thank you for understanding how much this mission means to me. Just know that I love and miss you all. I want to hear how preschool is going, kids. Gary, I miss hearing you sing in the shower." A long pause follows, as she blocks out the memory of what happened to Everett. She can't tell them about it yet.

"Okay! Time for work. Send me videos. Bye!"

Susan blows kisses into her private holomon, stops the video and hits send. Tiny doubts creep into her jumbled thoughts. Has she made the right decision coming here? Withholding information about Everett's death can't be helped at this time. Lt. Gen. Peters has issued a strict gag order over the events, pending the results of a full investigation. Sadly, the young technician has no relatives back home. His eagerness to help in a critical situation cost him his life.

Subdued melancholy creeps into Susan's mood. The Mars mission is supposed to be a life-changing experience. A positive one. Instead, the crew is already dealing with not only an unexplained death, but the possible culpability of an alien race. Veronica, whose rooms are right next to Susan's, left a few minutes ago for the Starlight Diner, a short walk from the colony's dorms. Susan heads out the door herself, following signs on the walls which direct her to the eatery. The rest of the mission's crew is seated, enjoying a fresh meal, something they haven't had in months. Susan loads her tray up with a huge serving of biscuits and gravy, then joins them at their table.

"I wish I could have saved him." Veronica can't believe that Everett is gone-just like that. She looks to her crewmates for an answer, but they have none. Susan tries to ease her distress as she picks up a fork.

"V-there is absolutely nothing you could have done out there to protect Everett."

"Thanks, Susan." Veronica smiles blandly. "It's really getting to me. I keep seeing his face."

"Let's try to concentrate on the reasons we were all chosen to come to Mars." Commander Newman reminds her crew.

"Each of us will be contributing to IVOSS's continued growth and success. It's not going to be easy, but we will rise to the challenge." Olivia stands and asks if anyone wants to explore the complex with her. Nick pushes back his chair, deciding to join her.

"I'll come with you. Let me get a to-go cup of java really quick." They walk over to the automated beverage machine.

"The coffee here is stout. Good thing. After what happened out there..." Olivia is still shaken by yesterday's events.

"I know what you mean," Nick says. "I had a hard time sleeping last night. I couldn't get the image of Everett out of my head, either. If you are up to some company tonight, I'm available. Our assignments don't start for a few days, yet." His hazel eyes hold Olivia's with a hint of promise.

"I'd like that." Oliva's reply brings the disarming grin to Nick's face that always gives her butterflies.

Maybe tonight is the night we take the next step. He acts like he feels the same way as I do. I am so ready to have his hands on me.

Ten minutes later, Susan excuses herself from the table. She has a meeting with IVOSS's medical examiner, Dr. Charles Lee, who will be performing a detailed autopsy of Everett's body. Outside the diner, a row of high-tech Segways await riders. Stepping onto one, she voices a command, "Destination-hospital morgue."

IVOSS is completely enclosed due to the risk of death from sustained exposure to Mars' thin atmosphere. All departments and living quarters are within fairly close proximity to each other. Each structure has a supply of solar-charged spacesuits. Humans can survive up to seventy-two hours on the planetary surface from within one.

The colony is built to be impregnable by the threat of a breach, partially protected within rock formations which comprise a portion of their design. However, additional safeguards have been implemented. International mass production of solar-powered spacesuits on Earth was a huge plus in continued settlement of the red planet. Technology keeps advancing at record speeds.

As she rides the self-driven scooter, Susan looks out the floor-to-ceiling breakproof windows, placed at twenty-foot intervals. The planetary surface is as calm as a pond at dusk. It's hard to believe it was heavily besieged by a record-setting dust storm yesterday. A slight movement under a large rock outcropping catches her eye. She commands the scooter to slowly approach the window for a better look.

That looks like an animal out there. Impossible!

Whatever it is stops to turn toward her, as if it knows she is watching.

I'm imagining it. But...

She watches the unknown figure until it suddenly disappears into the camouflage of the surroundings. The largest life forms discovered thus far on Mars still require the use of high-powered magnification. Nothing larger than a pin head has been confirmed. Still, she thinks again, more stubbornly this time...

I know what I saw.

Chapter Eleven-The Autopsy

Susan remains at the window a few more minutes, closely scrutinizing the terrain, but after nothing else appears, she heads for the medical center.

"Nice to meet you, Dr. Dorfmeyer." Dr. Lee is small in stature with straight black hair and intense brown eyes. He bows slightly, shaking Susan's hand, his grip firm.

"IVOSS is growing rapidly. Your arrival will ease the med clinic's workload. I'm sorry about the very tragic death of technician Everett Pickens." Dr. Lee motions for Susan to have a seat in his office. She chooses the one closest to his desk and accepts an offer of coffee.

"Thank you." Susan notices quite a few credentials hang on the otherwise bare walls. She is well-aware of his intellectual and surgical abilities. Dr. Lee, a legend within the CNSA, helped to pioneer an international med/surg center on the largest lunar outpost. His groundbreaking research and development while working in weightless environments continues to be of immense benefit. Since the colony requires a medical examiner, Dr. Lee graciously volunteers his services.

"I hope you don't mind if I join you for the autopsy?" Susan takes a sip of coffee, somewhat nervously.

"Everett's death was so quick. He appeared to be in excellent health from the looks of his file which I read last night. What do you make of it?"

"That's what I hope to find out. Come with me, please." The physicians enter the morgue. At the rear of the room, the examiner opens an air lock door. They step into a separate, rectangular enclosure which contains one large window. Susan observes an individual step outside from a second airlock exit, suited up, and exposed to the Martian atmosphere.

The medical examiner wants a test completed on the equipment Everett was wearing at the time of the incident.

"We sanitized the victim's spacesuit and helmet last night," he fills Susan in on what's happening. " Zero anomalies were detected in our diagnostics lab. My assistant, Sean, has offered to reenact the exposure event."

Dr. Lee is unaware of certain debriefing details revealed by the hanger's crew and Quantum One's crew. Claims of an alien ship landing and possibly prompting Everett's horrible death. Lt. Gen. Peters and First Lt. Hamilton, who conducted individual interviews, immediately issued a gag order to assure an impartial autopsy. Withholding information is starting to be their thing. No need to spark unnecessary panic.

"I'm unable to duplicate the harsh storm effects, but can at least test all suit functions," Dr. Lee continues. "You are most welcome to join me while I dictate the autopsy results. I only request that you hold any questions until I'm done recording."

After providing flawless suit performance and bio data back to the morgue computer terminals, Sean reenters the morgue.

"I had no problems out there, doctor." Sean gets some help removing the suit and shakes hands with Susan. "Morning, I'm Sean, the doc's guinea pig." Infectious laughter fills the room.

"I don't know about you guys, but I'm starving—again!" Sean's stomach gurgles loudly. "It has been a few hours since breakfast." Other than different facial features and hair color, Sean is the exact height and weight that Everett was, which is why the coroner asked him to perform the spacesuit test run.

"Thanks, Sean." Dr. Lee claps his assistant on the back. "Go eat."

Susan follows behind to prepare for the autopsy. Both don PPE. She notices the morgue has no cameras, unlike the rest of the colony. Humans retain the right to privacy while their final causes of death are determined. Ironic, in a sense, because almost every other area of the colony is monitored, providing various live feeds via IVOSS intranet. Autopsy results will eventually be made public, but never recorded. Per colony rules, they are required after every death, due to any number of risks which citizens have chosen to live under. Results can, if necessary, be delayed, pending further investigation.

Everett's body, obtained from the morgue's freezer drawer, waits silently on a wide stainless-steel table across the room. The corpse is covered with a white sheet. Dr. Lee rolls a hydraulic surgical tray next to the table. Various sharp instruments glint in the bright overhead lighting. Susan is reminded of the eight-week FBI postmortem externship she took part in during medical school. At that time, she was seriously considering a career in criminal forensic medicine.

The memory of it makes her shudder. It was the aftereffect of too many brutal cases which caused her to switch gears and specialize in reproductive advancement. The autopsies she took part in sickened her. All the decedents were victims of violent crime; a few, heartbreakingly, small children. She vowed to help advance the proliferation of life instead of investigating why and by what method people die.

Dr. Lee tests a mouthpiece which dangles from his headset. Wall-mounted speakers will broadcast the details.

"Testing one, two, three." The coroner's dictation is live and crystal clear.

"Sol day 210. LST 11:00. This is Dr. Charles Lee, IVOSS medical examiner. I am joined this morning by Dr. Susan Dorfmeyer. Commencing autopsy on technician Everett Scott Pickens. A 23-year-old Caucasian male. Health history is negative for any chronic disease or disorders. Right clavicle breakage as a teenager. Family history unknown as patient was adopted. No medications other than multivitamins. No recent onset of a new illness prior to his death."

The examiner pauses to glance at his tableside companion before pulling the sheet off of Everett. His corpse is pallid, the skin almost waxy in appearance. Susan watches intently as Lee slowly walks around the table, observing from afar before moving in close.

"The decedent is observed to have numerous petechial hemorrhages on the neck and face, indicative of asphyxia." Dr. Lee lifts Everett's eyelids up, one by one. "Conjunctivae have the same condition." Susan stays near but not in the way.

"No other signs of external trauma are noted on the decedent's body." Dr. Lee pulls down a transparent, protective screen from overhead. The two doctors shield themselves behind it while automated X-ray and CT machines move in to take a series of images. After a minute, the results are viewable on a large holomon.

"X-rays reveal a prior clean breakage of the decedent's right clavicle. CT images are conclusive for a massive stroke in the left posterior cerebellum. We will now approach to begin dissection."

Susan watches him lift a scalpel from the tray. He makes the traditional "Y" cut into Everett's pale torso, beginning from the top of both shoulders and meeting just below the breastbone. Past the stiffness of rigor mortis, the layers of skin, fat, and muscle yield to the pressure of the blade with zero resistance. The incision is then continued down to the top of the pubic bone. Susan takes a deep breath as she inches even closer. It's been years since she stood in and or/ assisted at autopsies.

"Evisceration of organs, followed by dissections will be conducted next."

Dr. Lee removes the cardiorespiratory block and places it on a stainless-steel counter. Cross slices of tissue are transferred to dishes. Their fleshy contents glisten like moist pieces of pink salmon under a seafood buffet light. Smaller specimens will be placed under high-powered microscopes for examination.

Susan looks at the digital clock on the wall as it tics off the small increments of Martian metric time. It seems like she has been on the red planet for longer than two days. Time *feels* different now. As if things are out of sync. The dictation brings her focus back to the task at hand.

"Initial assessments of organ samples reveal nothing abnormal. Semi-automated dissection of the decedent's brain will be the last procedure performed." Lee's voice softens with a slight air of finality. He steps back a few paces as does Dorfmeyer.

Cables with various instruments designed to saw and eviscerate drop down over the autopsy table, poised directly over Everett's head. His ashen face has been covered with a light, cotton cloth. The torso yawns open like a shallow grave, its absence of internal organs stark and sobering.

It doesn't take long for Susan to think she observes a slight, repetitive lifting up of the facial cloth, as if Everett has suddenly come back to life and blows puffs of breath beneath it. She blinks a few times to rid herself of the illusion.

Both doctors solemnly watch automated instruments cut the anterior sheath away from the cranium. Next, a low-pitched saw whines into Everett's skull. In a matter of seconds, the cranial plates are removed, and the brain is completely exposed. Dr. Lee painstakingly eviscerates and withdraws the glistening organ. He places it onto a weighted scale. Something is glaringly amiss.

Everett's brain weighs less than normal because it has no frontal or occipital lobes. They are missing, sans, absent.

What the actual fuck. Susan's inner voice can't believe what her outer eyes are seeing.

"The...decedent's brain..." Dr. Lee hesitates..."has been anatomically altered. The lobes have been removed with clean sites of separation from the cerebellum, as if they have undergone cold cauterization. There is no evidence of prior clotting in those areas. This critical anomaly did not appear on the CT scan. I'm not sure why."

Several thin slices of the cerebellum are obtained. They look like cross sections of giant pallid mushrooms, ready to be chopped down for a salad topping. Probably much less palatable, even with the addition of blue cheese dressing and crunchy, homemade croutons.

"There is evidence of a fatal subdural hematoma in the posterior left cerebellum. This appears to be why the decedent lost consciousness and eventually bled to death. Exterior indications support my opinion."

"In regard to the absence of lobes, there is no prior instance, to my knowledge, of this ever being documented in a human being before. It looks to have transpired posthumously."

Dr. Lee pauses to clear his throat.

"The decedent's death was from fatal brain hemorrhage. As to how the brain was altered, I cannot determine the method by which it was performed or for what purpose."

The medical examiner looks at Susan. His dark eyes are dead serious. She feels a pit in her stomach.

Chapter Twelve-Rendezvous

Olivia steps out from the hot shower and puts on a thin cotton robe. Her quarters are kept at a comfortable sixty-nine degrees. Most maintenance and utility jobs are performed by androids. They handle housekeeping chores and also manage surveillance in the security center. Advancements have been made in their ability to take on higher level functions.

Humanoid battery life is increased due to a combination of photovoltaic and solar technology. AI voices and movements are for the most part fairly realistic, at times difficult to distinguish from a human. However, if battery life falls to less than ten percent, a robot's voice inflection suffers serious degradation, becoming similar to a sinister Vincent Price singing "The Monster Mash" in slow motion. AI's have the trademark "A" on the front of their shirts to denote status, followed by a human name and number. When unclothed, the same designation is stamped on silicone chest plates. If one is in doubt, robots are programmed to automatically remove a shirt for inspection when ordered to do so.

The mission commander walks over to the studio kitchen and punches a button on the wall, causing a beverage shelf to slide out. It's loaded with various cups and glasses. She selects a wine glass, lifting it to look at the glean of sharply faceted sides. A chilled bottle of Chardonnay sits in an ice bucket. Imported, of course, and left as a welcome gift from a small winery on Mars which stocks some of Earth's finest wines and, for the less discerning, more commonly marketed wines, too. The sound of it falling into her glass is soothing, like witnessing a miniature waterfall at eye level. She takes a couple of sips, savoring the semi-dry flavor that only improves as it makes contact with her palate. She licks her lips and sighs.

Now, all I need is some engaging company. As in, a man.

As if on cue, she hears a soft knock at the door. Olivia crosses over and looks through the peephole. It's Nick. Her heart skips a beat. It's amazing how he makes her feel so alive. She opens the door a crack, looks at him with flashing green eyes and cheeks rosy from the hot shower. She allows the robe to gap open, revealing the soft curve of firm breasts, drawing his eyes down appreciatively.

"May I help you, Mr. Johansen?" Olivia's face is just as beautiful without makeup since she is blessed with gorgeous skin and naturally long, dark lashes. She blinks them, a little too innocently, at Nick.

"Yes ma'am-I believe you can." Nick takes the bait. His gaze moves to meet hers, dark brows knitted in mock seriousness.

"I received a report of a young woman in need of company. Are you *the* Olivia Newman?"

"Yes," Olivia swings the door all the way open. Nick steps inside. She barely gets it shut before he's on her, pushing her gently against the wall. Olivia's heart beats more quickly. She buries her face into the sweet spot where Nick's powerful shoulder meets his chest. Breathing in his strong scent increases her desire.

"You smell so good. I'm afraid I can't compete. All I used was lavender body wash in the shower." Olivia's moist lips pout. She's driving Nick crazy and is well aware of it.

"Mmmmm-I noticed. A man loves a woman when they're fresh out of a shower." His voice turns husky. "All sweet and clean, but still a little wet down below."

"Goddamn, Nick, you know just what to say..." Olivia shakes her head, releasing hair from the messy bun she had put in after showering. The still moist tendrils frame her glowing face as Nick peels off the robe and picks her up in his strong arms. He walks toward the bedroom, kissing her all over ardently.

"I've got to have you now." Nick places her on the bed and watches her recline back like a tigress. He eyes her gorgeous body while he undresses slowly. Olivia doesn't move. She watches him, taking in the gorgeous 6' 2-inch physique. He lifts a form-fitting T-shirt over his head, messing up thick, dark hair. Then, the jeans and briefs come off. She gasps softly when she sees him entirely naked. He climbs on top of her, his eyes never leaving hers and slides down her supple body, gently opening smooth-as-silk legs with one hand.

"You're beautiful. I've been dreaming about this for a long time." Nick's arousal is evident. He takes his time with her, performing painstakingly thorough oral sex. Her body shakes and trembles as it's racked by back-to-back orgasms. She reaches down and grasps his manhood.

"I want this. Now."

When their lovemaking is over, they both fall back onto the pristine white sheets of the queen bed, feeling destressed and amazingly relaxed in each other's presence. Their coupling was going to happen, sooner than later. This is the longest mission they've been on together. The mutual attraction has been present since the moment they first met, so neither are surprised at where it has led.

'I'm saving you for last, Olivia.'

What the hell? Where did that come from?

Olivia shudders. The vague memory of having heard someone say that to her recently is unsettling. She pushes it out of her mind. It's all about Nick now.

"Nick, that was wonderful. And, just what I needed." Olivia raises herself out of the crook of Nick's arm to give him a deep kiss.

"You're not kidding. I needed it too. I've been pent up as hell after what happened to that kid, Everett. What do you think the autopsy results will tell us?"

"I have no idea. Susan will help us figure it out. We all saw what happened to him. It was so quick." Olivia frowns and strokes Nick's face.

"Would you like some wine? I didn't have a chance to offer you any." She looks at him amusingly, deciding to focus on them.

"I'd love some." He watches her slide out of bed, not shy to walk around stark naked in front of him. Their intimacy has emboldened her, and it arouses him again. A minute later, she returns with the wine bottle and two glasses on a tray.

"Here you go," Olivia smiles demurely, sitting down on the bed. "Cheers, Nick."

"Cheers, Olivia." Their glasses clink and they both take a sip together. A comfortable pause follows before the commander continues. She turns on the live feed holmon via voice control. Various shots of the colony instantly load.

"I received orders a few minutes before you came over. The two of us and Devon will be joining the Reusable Transport Department. There's a lot of work to be done to improve sustainable craft production and fuel development. Devon is so gifted. I have a lot of confidence in his capabilities. Susan and V will bring a lot to the table in their areas of medical care and crop production. I can't wait to see what we accomplish together."

Nick nods his head in agreement. He runs his finger up between Olivia's breasts, cups her chin in his hands and kisses her lips, softly.

"We've got a great team. I'm anxious to get to work. But first..." Nick takes the glass out of Olivia's hand. The live feed is the last thing on their minds.

Chapter Thirteen-Star Rejenitus

Mithra floats at the head of a smoldering, curved desk from within Star Rejenitus' command headquarters, located in the capitol city of Helenox. It exists on the massive star's northernmost location. The surface temperature averages close to 20,000 degrees. Solar geysers explode upward like dragons belching towering torches of fire. They expand the reach of a corona which resembles volcanic liquid lava, spewing an expanding crimson stain into the blackness and solitude of space.

Being impervious to heat and radiation, Reji have constructed the most advanced city in the Luxar Galaxy, sparking the envy of other solar-spawned races. Towering edifices tremble amidst undulating waves of infrared energy, yet still maintain structural integrity. Huge monoliths, unaffected by seemingly uninhabitable elements, pull power from the boiling stellar surface which fuels everything to do with Reji life functions, particularly interstellar space exploration.

Far off in the distance, gargantuan launch pads operate with atomic precision, able to catapult ships into the cosmos on a moment's notice. Mothership Rejenitus rests on the largest one, charging up for future missions; her massive underdecks absorb underground stores of hydrogen at a mindboggling rate. Smaller vessels rest on peripheral outposts, dotting the surface like burning polka dots.

Ringing the Luxar Galaxy is a continuous black abyss of unknown origin. The Syren waits like a silent sentinel for those who wish to learn the truth. Star Rejenitus, spawned from its bottomless depths at the dawn of universal creation, casts far-reaching flames out for all to behold, an eternal pyre of nuclear fusion.

Analysis of mankind's higher neuroprocessing is complete. Mithra provides an update. *I am pleased to report it possesses all necessary levels of consciousness required for upload to the Syren. Infiltration has commenced of the human popula-*

tion via two females who carry fetus hybrids within their fertile wombs. It was necessary to sacrifice one male specimen for examination, but his thoughts will never die. We now know the prognosis for propagation is excellent.

Humans have achieved intergalactic space travel and colonization of different worlds, albeit their efforts are quite primitive in comparison to ours. Our teams were able to decipher sufficient amounts of alien data when we intercepted their vessel. Billions of these creatures exist on a planet called Earth. When the hybrids mature on Mars, colonists of the red planet will learn the reason for our invasion. After that, having hopefully succeeded in converting open minds, we can set our sights on a voluntary exodus of Earth's population.

Remember, once the hybrids come of age, Reji genetic material will be ready for immediate and rapid introduction into the adult population via additional methods. Humans are unlike any we have mated with before. They are highly intuitive and emotional beings who long for eternal life after death. Reji will help them achieve that, when they so desire, by replacing their DNA with ours. Let us monitor the outcome on Mars before we expand to the blue planet they call home.

Mithra's telepathic update receives good reaction. Space Command board members nod bulbous heads in excitement. Glowing eyes jiggle like black olives in bowls of jello. The primary objective of the Reji race is to enlighten other species in regard to what eternity is. Any hybrid offspring eventually revert to Reji beings, with the exception of cloaking their bodies in whatever alien skin has been infiltrated. This method has worked well for them over the eons. It remains imperative to expand their numbers, ensuring the enlightenment of as many qualifying species as possible. In time, newly indoctrinated races lose their original features. It's intellect over physical attributes. Our memories define us. Not our looks.

Zorn and Cygorg, Mithra's top assistants, float beside him. Other Reji in attendance watch an image formulate in the center of the room. Olivia and Susan are shown. Mithra feels a strange sensation upon seeing Olivia's face again. What is it about this one that sets her apart from the many others he has had relations with?

Gestation length should be approximately the same as earthlings, as will reaching puberty. We must be patient while data is gathered on their growth progression. In the meantime, other exploratory missions will commence. Reji have the ability to export vestiges of consciousness ensuring propagation on stars within our home galaxy and eventual migration to the Syren. At this time, you are released to your individual command posts to dispatch ships. May you have success in finding life forms to convert. Any waring species who seek to impede us will be destroyed.

Zorn and Cygorg remain behind after members pass through a shimmering wall as if it wasn't there, melting into the inferno. Their molten shapes wave like sea snakes swimming in ocean waters, eventually fading away into mountainous curtains of fire.

Cygorg, proceed to the main launch area to oversee preparations of Mothership Rejenitus. Zorn, come with me to the observation deck.

Mithra and Zorn float to the uppermost level of the building. The roof of the structure resembles a dilating iris. Overlapping panels slowly open in a counter-clockwise motion, revealing star-filled space, made visible through a dormant area of the boiling surface. Mithra's black orbs also expand as he scans the cosmos for alien vessels.

A tight cluster of dots appears in the upper right quadrant of the gargantuan aperture. Higher magnification reveals bright blue, crossbow-shaped ships headed toward the Luxar Galaxy. He and Zorn are able to discern the familiar "X" next to an image of a white dwarf star on the vessels' sides. The letter and star signify they are from the Xerusian Fleet, a rebel galactic race originating from a nearby galaxy on the brink of death known as Xerusa. Since their home stars are lacking in hydrogen, hostile Xerus frequently travel to other constellations, invading red dwarfs for seizures of much-needed fuel.

Mithra looks at Zorn and his black eyes deepen with ire. He will not allow another invasion to occur. Although it will take some time for the enemy to arrive, he will muster his warriors. A repeat invasion and loss of hydrogen fuel threatens Reji expansion efforts. This will not be tolerated.

Further camouflage all available stores. Utilize the largest of our cloaked stars to conceal additional reserves. You are my most capable officer, Zorn. If Reji warriors must be sacrificed to protect our supplies, then so be it. We must remain a mobile race at all costs.

The aperture shuts but the unblinking eyes of Mithra, never do.

Chapter Fourteen-Surprise Sickness

After the autopsy, Everett's body is wheeled out of the room for transport to the crematorium. Colonists are required to sign a pre directive on what is to be done with their remains if they pass away on Mars. Everett selected cremation. His pale corpse, already bloated and bearing numerous scars from the dissection procedure, lies under a sheet, as lifeless as a deer left to rot on the side of a sunbaked Arizona highway. One frigid arm silently slips off the steel gurney. Long, bony fingers hang over the white tiled floor, as if attempting to grasp a helping hand from some unknown, subterranean hero. A hero who will never materialize. Susan watches until the gurney turns the corner. Out of sight and out of mind. She wishes.

The Mars Memorial Mausoleum currently houses charred remains of two hundred brave scientific souls. Fearless pioneers who, at times, left former lives behind to further mankind's journey into the unknown. There are no below-ground burial plots. Inhabitants also have the option to send their intact remains into space, merging with stellar dust, or perhaps joining with primordial gases to form future super giants. From death to rebirth among the stars. Not a bad way to go out-literally.

Both doctors walk to the medical clinic, which is open daily from 8-7, LST. This is where colonists receive physical exams and other health-related care. Each physician will have rotating days off to do their own thing, be it additional research, recreation, or just staying in house binging on books and movies. Free time is one of life's most valuable commodities. Most people don't realize this until too late in life, rushing around like worker bees in a hive.

Susan meets lead psychiatrist, Dr. Earnest Sebastian, who, along with ancillary staff, support the mental health needs of residents. He's British, soft-spoken, and broadcasts weekly podcasts which boost morale. Next, Dr. Lee introduces Dr. Balabanov before returning to his office. The former IVOSS president speaks four languages, including impeccable English. Dr. Dorfmeyer accompanies him on late morning rounds, noting genuine compassion and thoroughness with his patients. They finish the last check of the morning.

"Lunch time, Dr. Dorfmeyer. I bet you're hungry."

"Yes! I'm told the food is quite good."

Self-cleaning round tables beckon inside the cafeteria. Each has a holocam hanging in the center, constantly displaying various live feeds. Bright light, some of it artificial, pours into and over the room. Workers and residents talk animatedly during a midday meal. After normal business hours, prompt, albeit impersonal food service, is provided by robots . The names on their shirts glow at night, as do blue irises, providing confirmation of internal AI synapses rather than genuine neurons capable of sentient thought.

Susan loads up a tray, surprised at how hungry she is. The doctors find seats at an open table. At first, the fish sandwich tastes delectable, but, after a few minutes, her stomach starts to feel slightly queasy. A hot belch comes up the back of her throat, forcing her to choke back a blast of acid-infused saliva.

I hardly ate anything for breakfast. What's with the sudden nausea? Maybe I should slow down and stop inhaling French fries. Lay off the ketchup.

Susan glances at Dr. Sebastian who sits on her left side. He's very tall from the waist up and has to direct his gaze downward at her. He smiles, revealing straight, white teeth.

What kind eyes he has. Susan thinks to herself. *He seems very easy to talk to. I might make an appointment with him. But first, I need a bathroom break.*

"Gentleman, it's been nice meeting you. I'm looking forward to working with the IVOSS medical team. If you'll excuse me, please. See you in the morning, Dr. Balabanov."

Susan stands and smiles at the men, quickly turning from the table in an effort to hide the fact that she feels sick to her stomach. She exits the cafeteria, rushing to the closest bathroom. The stall door bangs shut behind her. Beads of sweat break out on her forehead. Dropping to wobbly knees, she wretches violently, emptying her stomach of the lunch she just ate. Remnants swirl in the water before the automatic flush deposits fresh water.

What the hell have I done to get sick like this? I passed the pre-mission health assessment with flying colors.

She rips toilet paper off the roll using it to wipe drops of spittle that cling to her chin.

Shit, I sure didn't see that coming. I'd better lie down for an hour. Then I can send Gary and the kids another message. The door gets jerked open. Her reflection in the mirror is startling. She's white as a sheet. What if—

Hope I'm not pregnant.

The rogue thought creeps into her head as if nothing could prevent its admission.

No way. Gary had a vasectomy over two years ago. But throwing up sure reminds me of my pregnancy with Zoe. I was sick from day one. Ugh.

Dr. Dorfmeyer splashes cool water onto pale cheeks. It helps bring her back to reality. No need to panic.

I'm sure it was something I ate that just didn't agree with me. Nothing a few minutes rest won't cure.

Entering her dorm, Susan slides recycled work shoes off, easing back onto the comfortable bed.

My lids feel so heavy. Can't keep them open.

'Sleep, doctor. A deep, sonorous voice in her ear. '*Let me take you down memory lane. And show you a glimpse of the future.'*

Wiping unpleasant memories of morning sickness from her mind, Susan instead recalls the adoration she felt when Zoe was placed into her arms. Sleep creeps up on her musings.

I want another baby...so very badly.

Now fast asleep, effects of alien DNA already affecting hormonal patterns, preparing her for phenomenal changes. Laying the groundwork for new life from merged loins. Vivid dreams portend a wonderful future.

While Dr. Dorfmeyer snoozes, Olivia, Nick, and Devon report to the Reusable Transport Department, or RTD. John Largos heads the unit. He's eager for additional help.

"RTD is thrilled to have you join our team! We'll be starting off this afternoon with a tour followed by a Q & A session in the conference room. Sound good?"

John exudes loads of boisterous energy. His passion for continued development and deployment of reusable craft is evident as he shows off various rovers and rockets that await improvement suggestions from the newly expanded team.

Devon keenly eyes the largest of the rocket boosters while it undergoes various testing.

"How is the production of fuel from Martian microbes coming along? I know the process needs to be shortened. I've got a few ideas."

"Awesome! I can't wait to hear them." The annexed Rocket and Rover Prototype Building is next up on the tour. Hold on—let me take this call." John steps off to the side, his voice echoes in their ears as the doors to the department shut behind them, locking automatically. Only certain individuals are allowed access.

To their right, several groundbreaking rover designs go through a series of steering maneuvers. Next week, they'll be tested outside, finalizing use of an onboard system of water recycling. The latest manned helicopter prototype rests on a platform next to the rovers. Devon's voice reflects his excitement.

"I've been waiting to see this baby. She has redesigned lithium-ion battery packs and solar panels that can expand to capture a lot more energy!"

John catches up to the others and guides them through the facility, lecturing about the remaining prototypes. At the back of the building, he opens a set of locked double doors via a retina scan. Once inside the temperature-controlled room, Devon, Olivia , and Nick view ten hibernation pods, occupied with humans. The pods hiss and click intermittently, marking the passage of delayed aging on the reposing volunteers. All color is gone from their faces, slowed circulation is now directed in support of major organs. They appear to be dead. Yet, they live. The three crew members can't stop staring at them.

"This is the most important research of all. Fifteen Rhesus monkeys and four individuals have successfully come through trials aboard NASA's Gateway system. Now, it's being tested on humans here. Hibernation is poised to take man further into the cosmos. To go where no man has gone before."

Largos points to a large picture of the Enterprise's bridge with Captain Kirk at its helm. Dr. Spock stands next to him.

"It's just the beginning." John says. "Trekkies and space lovers have been waiting a long time for this."

Chapter Fifteen-Settling In

The merging of Q-One's team with IVOSS's research and development departments has gone well. So well, the crew may decide to remain on the colony indefinitely. Devon and John stay busy with other scientists, brainstorming different techniques to speed up conversion of the Martian atmosphere into high performance rocket oxyfuel. Magnetic shield prototypes being developed demonstrate an effective capability for shielding Mars from the sun. Surface temperature will increase because the atmosphere won't be stripped, enhancing terraforming efforts.

Veronica plans are to introduce several greenhouse processes designed to enrich the regolith growing medium. Monthly crop yield should double. Dandelions have done remarkably well on the red planet. Every part of the flower is edible or drinkable. A toast was made to Ray Bradbury after the first batch of dandelion wine was manufactured on Mars. Golden is good. And long-lasting. Presently, two huge greenhouses produce fruits and vegetables that rival organic equivalents grown on Earth.

Companion animals are not allowed, although that is set to change soon. A recently passed referendum will permit one pet per household. Mankind is still trying to adapt to the harsh environment themselves. Most of the colony's lab animals are thriving but some have had issues. Domestic creatures will be no different. A small vet clinic is being constructed with state-of-the-art features. When the first companion animals arrive, staff will already be in place. Long-ago proven to be wonderful stress reducers, beloved small creatures are sure to provide much morale.

Olivia, in bed since ten o'clock after a productive day, finds herself wide awake staring at the ceiling of her bedroom. The glow from the bathroom night light provides a dim view of the room along with the nightstand clock's blue digital display. She sees the glint of her silver locket on the nightstand. Its polished casing glimmers like a coin submerged in water. A small picture of her younger brother rests inside, taken before his terminal cancer diagnosis. The heart wrenching loss haunts her daily. A weighted chain of sorrow that, at times, drags her down into a dark, depressing abyss. Usually, she can climb out. Tonight, however, being so far from his peaceful gravesite, which she often visited, it's extra painful. Her fingers pop the dainty locket open. Shiloh's little face is smiling, barely illuminated in the soft light.

God, I miss you, little bro. Remember when we slept on top of the roof and watched shooting stars all night? You told me you wanted to grow up to be an astronaut. I know it's not fair what happened. Researchers are so close to developing a cure for brain cancer. People, especially kids, won't have to suffer from it anymore, like you did. Just know, I'm living your wish for you, bud. I bet heaven is awesome. Love you.

Olivia wipes hot tears from her eyes, feeling unusually warm. Almost feverish. A thin layer of sweat coats her arms.

I'm sure the thermostat is set to auto. Man, 'bout ready to piss myself, too. I just went before bed—jeez.

She stands up, slightly groggy. Flashes of a dream suddenly come back to her. Bits and pieces. Bright lights. A feeling of helplessness. Nothing concrete. Only a vague recollection of an unfamiliar location and being in the presence of something foreign. After a few seconds trying to grasp more details, she gives up and goes to the restroom.

I wonder if this pattern of waking is because I know I'm five days late for my period. Maybe starting a low-estrogen-dose birth control wasn't such a great idea. But my headaches were worsening and it's what the doctor recommended.

Returning to sit on the side of her bed, Olivia impulsively pulls a nightstand drawer open. There, sitting in the glow of artificial blue light are birth control pills. When she opens the package, she notices quite a few have been skipped.

Shit. Why the hell didn't I set a notification to keep up on these? Nick didn't use protection. It was the last thing on our minds. Damn, I could use another dose of his "therapy". It's all I can think about.

Olivia sighs as she pulls the covers up under her chin. Sleep returns, her thoughts swirling around the man she has fallen head over heels in love with, the knowledge of skipped contraceptive doses no longer pressing.

The following morning, Veronica, whose dorm is in the same building as Olivia's, sends a video message to her mom, telling her thus far the mission is everything she hoped for. Everett's passing is omitted from the update. News won't get back to Earth until official autopsy results are released. No need to get mom worked up. She wishes real time video was possible, but it hasn't been perfected yet. Recordings have to suffice.

"I've joined the crop production team, Mom! Mars is proving to be a richer growth environment than originally thought. With supplemental synthetic additives we'll be growing more in the next year than the prior five! Plus, massive ice reserves, far below the surface, are going to provide all the water we could ever need for a very long time. When I come home, I'll bring you a bottle of Ocampo wine. It's named after a crater here and was brewed with Martian ice water! I know Ocampo is where you were born. Miss you so much, mom. Especially those bomb enchiladas."

V makes a heart symbol with her hands, then blows a kiss into the lens, smiling broadly. After sending the message, she walks to a window, gazing out at nothing in particular. The morning air is moderately hazy. Several rocket hangers tower in the distance.

Guilty feelings flood her head when she remembers, for the umpteenth time, what she had to tell her mom, Isla, three years ago. A gynecologist found the reason for severe monthly cramping and abnormally heavy menstrual flow was due to advanced endometriosis blocking both fallopian tubes. An ultrasound also detected a large uterine tumor. The pain had become so severe Veronica opted for surgery. It was decided to perform a complete hysterectomy.

Although Isla was devastated, she resolved to remain positive, for her daughter's sake, as usual. Veronica hasn't ruled out adoption, if and when the time is right. After her mark is made on Mars.

I wish I could hop in my car and drive to mom's house. So thankful she has good neighbors. God protect her, please. V heads out the apartment door, deep in thought.

Far out on the horizon dust devils race toward chiseled rock monoliths. They reach dark bases and immediately disintegrate, as if a magician's sleight of hand has been used to make them disappear. Now you see them. Now you don't. Dried riverbeds, where raging water once flowed, carve indelible patterns on the parched terrain. Each one holds a wealth of knowledge. Did alien creatures once travel on Martian land and water? Did they perhaps deploy solar-sailed vehicles capable of more than just movement? And, if alien larger life forms once existed, what happened to them? Maybe they left a world which was dying. As the millennium progress, questions like these that keep mankind up at night will be answered, by a select few people or by many. Usually, it's the former preceding the latter. Scientists who dare to challenge the status quo.

Within walking distance, the colony's A&E Dept. rises four stories into the air. It's one of the largest complexes, understandably. Food production and engineering are the backbones of prolonged space travel. Improvements in crop management mean that eventually, supplemental assistance will no longer be required from Earth. Or at least greatly reduced. In fact, as time steadily marches into the future, the *desire* for return trips to the blue planet, will replace the *need*. After Mars has been fully developed, man will proceed to conquer the mysteries of other celestial bodies. And so on, and so on. It will never end. Infinity means forever.

Chapter Sixteen-Expect the Unexpected

Xerus will stop at nothing to steal hydrogen under their intimidating commander, Vane. The Xerusa Galaxy, a mere ten light years away from the Luxar Galaxy, is dying. Only one white dwarf remains. The others collapsed into bottomless black holes. Saving Amorpheus, the lone surviving star where he and his ancestors hail from, is paramount. There are times, however, when Vane chooses to ignore the consequences of occasional neglect.

Under strict orders, Xerusian ships, led by Warship Xenith, are planning another hostile theft of fuel from Star Rejenitus. Xerus resemble Reji in appearance, with the exception of possessing a red pall to their vaporous forms along with huge, red eyes instead of black. They boast a much larger fleet than the one commandeered by Mithra. It includes carrier vessels which travel piggyback-style, designed to transport gargantuan stores of hydrogen.

One advantage Rejis hold over Xerus is a highly advanced cloaking ability which Vane is intensely envious of. Xenith's fleet can scramble signals but never becomes completely invisible. What good are conveyance ships if hydrogen reserves cannot be located? The only way to learn site coordinates is to threaten alien leaders with the massacre of citizens. The majority of Rejis exist within the burning red dwarf's production capital, Helenox. Vane will not hesitate to drop paralytic gas onto strategic areas, an offensive tactic his scientists perfected eons ago that results in great loss of life.

During a prior war campaign, underground supplies of hydrogen were discovered, and removed from the star's on-site reserves. Since that transpired, Vane learned from recognizant reports that Reji moved critical hydrogen supplies to nearby stars and are able to cloak those stars in obscurity. Mithra has warned Vane to never attempt an invasion again. However, the Luxar Galaxy is just too close to resist a repeat attack. Amorpheus must replenish its fuel supply.

Vane knows Mithra is able to view his formidable star fleet. When faced with annihilation, Reji citizens are sure to reveal where fuel reserves are hidden. He is prepared to kill however many inhabitants to accomplish the mission.

Xerus, like the majority of alien beings, use high functioning brains to communicate via telepathy. Vane floats inside Xenith's command hub, observing detailed attack plans with his top three warriors. Bulbous, red eyes rise periodically to scan the cosmos racing by at mind-boggling speeds. Xerus and Reji can slow visual perception down to observable levels with manipulation of optic pathways. Hyper-tuned cells make up the entire posterior pole of their eyes. Incredibly dense optic nerves contain gene variants, enhancing sight functions. Vane addresses his top assistants.

Doma, Mirt, you will each direct your ships toward Helenox. Plan your attack to take place when Mothership Rejenitus is off galivanting around the cosmos, looking for converts. We are aware Reji possess one track minds in regard to sharing secrets of the Syren to other worthy civilizations. Their self-serving schemes will be thwarted when we target and kill beloved Reji family members. Mithra's incessant claims about immortality are ridiculous. We have witnessed the decay of Xerusa's stars, one by one, until only Amorpheus remains, yet have NEVER been offered assistance.

Rejis fill other races with false hopes of eternal salvation within a black tomb. All we care about is stealing their fuel. Vane gestures with his transparent appendages for effect.

They claim knowledge of learning why the universe exists once passage into the Syren occurs, yet no Xerus have ever returned from **our** *galaxy's black holes after death. Remains during Casting Ceremonies are sent to them and that's the end. The knowledge we possess points to eternal nothingness.*

Our mission is of the utmost importance. In the event you are faced with death, remember the Xerusian oath to our home star, Amorpheus. She is facing mortal gravitational collapse, leading to extinction of your loved ones. Hydrogen stores must be replenished, or she will not survive the next millennium. The space atomic clock is ticking. Achieve that which provides assurance your families will live for millions of years in their home galaxy. We don't want to migrate, however, the option remains on the table as a last-ditch effort.

Jericho's scarlet orbs narrow. He is a ruthless warrior, having enjoyed great success in prior battles. He doesn't take pleasure in killing others, but survival necessitates it. At home, his extended family awaits the return of energy stores needed for sustenance. The thought of having to leave their home star is terrifying to them. Most have no desire to become a migratory species. Jericho plans on completing the mission. He listens intently to orders to remain with Vane.

Remember to deploy your blue heat shields. The temperature on Star Rejenitus is much hotter than it is on Amorpheus for our star is dying and grows cooler. Utilize every method of attack you have perfected. Your ships need to land near the Reji command headquarters during one of their meetings. Breach the HQ building and capture Mithra first. My hatred toward him is indescribable. He dared to insult my family. We have lost warriors because of his unwillingness to share energy stores. Well, if he does not reveal the coordinates of those cloaked coffers, he will have his own family massacred. And that will be just the beginning.

Vane floats in and out between their bodies. He raises his right hand. They raise theirs in return and prepare to recite the battle oath of obedience. Apparently, many species besides man recite oaths to pump themselves up. Not surprising. Even if it is telepathically.

I am a Xeru. My home star is Amorpheus. I vow to fight for her survival in the face of all risk, even death. There is only the here and now. There is only TODAY! If I should perish, it will be for the Xerusian race. Long live Xerus!

The three warriors bring alien hands up to meet Vane's. They glow like the embers of a dying fire, lighting the forward cabin of the star ship. Only their huge, crimson eyes glow brighter. A smokey redness bleeds into the air, becoming so dense that the four Xerus become obscured in the thick haze. Their arms fall and they lower enlarged heads to the floor of the craft. A silence hangs in the module.

Suddenly, Vane engages in a high-pitched death chant. The Xerus raise their heads and begin to follow each other in a frenzied circle that increases in speed. Incinerator orbs burn like hot coals in a furnace, throwing out sparks of vibrant color. Vane notices something out of the corner of his eye, causing him to cease the fervid war dance in its tracks. The view from the huge port-side window is entirely blocked by a massive ship. It's Mothership Rejenitus. Her sides shimmer like endless ripples in a melted pool of gold.

Vane's one-word reaction invades the minds of his cohorts.

Fuck!

Chapter Seventeen-Let's Make a Deal

A bright light permeates the interior of Xenith, whose trajectory is on the verge of being altered. Vane's officers halt their return to peripheral vessels. Jericho, sensing trouble, smacks a red button at eye level, which succeeds in deploying the fleet's safety shields. The defense maneuver is too late, however. Mothership Rejenitus has tethered herself to the smaller and subpar Xerusian vessel.

Reji ships advance with cloaked stealth, quickly launching mega-ionized sheaths designed to manipulate enemy vessels. Mothership Rejenitus sabotages alien flight software, programming a revised course. Quite brilliant and very effective. Rather demoralizing for a small-time command ops leader.

Vane sends an enraged hologram message to Mithra, for he is well aware of Reji attack methods. Good thing the other half of his attack force has already landed on Helenox. The governmental seat is ripe for a takeover, with Mithra being absent, carelessly leaving idiots in charge.

Red spider veins pulse under pink, translucent skin on his thick neck. The Xerusian anthem plays on repeat in the background. His ancillary force is also livid; a few float up to join Vane, forming a protective circle around him, for they have sworn vapid lives in his service.

What have you done to my ships, Mithra? I need them to steal fuel from YOU! Helenox headquarters is under seize on Star Rejenitus. You had best remove yourself from my vessel or I'll be forced to submit a most dire order. Isn't the Reji governmental seat next to your parental home? I will have them all killed. My fleet outnumbers yours and however many of my ships you manipulate, there will be too many for you in the long run.

Mithra obligingly appears in his own, not-as-vivid hologram message, for Xerus have surpassed Reji in that science. Although slightly grainy, it's still clear enough to be seen and its occupant understood. His black eyes bore through the interior of Xenith's flight deck, searching for the commander.

Vane, Mothership Rejenitus is capable of destroying your fleet, ship by ship. Today, however, they will only be redirected to a different location until I have had my say. First off, your flight software is in need of serious upgrades. It was very easily sabotaged. Reji have yet to find a system that we cannot manipulate. Talk to your developers.

Jericho prevents Vane from lunging at the image. His face is now contorted with rage. Mithra, moving on from the initial insult, waves long, thin hands in a gesture of supplication.

Secondly, I have a proposition for you. Hear me out before you self-destruct from anger.

The pulsing throbs slowly diminish on Vane's neck as he gradually calms down. He's always been a sucker for deals. Gullible citizens on Amorpheus somehow continue to worship every move he makes, idolizing him in verse and artwork, even though he has a well-known history of bartering away fuel for bigger and faster warships.

Crimson eyes turn a more pale shade of red; nostril slits slow their rate of respiration. His curiosity is definitely peaked. The tense atmosphere in the command hub eases.

Mithra's wavy image improves in clarity. Onyx-hued orbs shift between Vane and his aids then halt on the commander, endeavoring to hold his attention span, which is known to be less than ideal.

Xenith's fleet will be guided to a young Reji star named Pyron which burns within the Luxar Galaxy. It has remained cloaked until now. She possesses enough stores of hydrogen to prolong Xerus' existence for at least 100 million years. I offer this vast supply in exchange for your release of Reji headquarters, and a promise that you will seek fuel replenishment elsewhere in the cosmos. Both of our armies suffered a loss of life that was far too high in prior battles. Does this not sound like a reasonable resolution, Vane? You will observe Pyron shortly.

By this time, Vane has regained complete composure. His eyes lighten even more and have an almost friendly expression to them. Xerus and Reji alike have lower extremities that are not as discernible as their upper bodies. His gnarled fists noticeably relax an enraged clench.

Mithra, how gracious of you to propose such a generous offer. Although it is maddening to know you have altered the course of my fleet away from inevitable conflict, the prospect of viewing star Pyron is very enticing. Keep talking.

We are but a few constellations away. Mithra coaxes Vane as if speaking to a child. *Advance to the window so you can take in a favorable view. Your other ships' occupants will see Pyron, also. Our descent will drop in quite close, enabling you to make out landing zones scattered all over the star, albeit most loading sites have been erected on its southern hemisphere. This is where Pyron's greatest fusion takes place. These locations are marked with huge black obelisks. Xerus will be able to load and transport fuel as many times as you like, for the star will remain uncloaked. In return, you must agree to abandon your invasion of Star Rejenitus immediately.*

Mithra continues to woo Vane. What he doesn't tell him is that he is lying about his knowledge of hydrogen stores on Pyron. It could be a lot. It could be a little. All he knows for sure is the star presently exhibits an extremely high amount of nuclear fusion. Many things can affect star life, so nothing is actually guaranteed. He can sense the Xerusian commander is on the verge of backing down.

Vane and his men approach Xenith's floor-to-ceiling window. Below, Star Pyron spins on its own axis, in the throes of violent atomic activity. Amorpheus could sure use this gifted source of life! The landing sites are easily spotted, each one is able to receive and launch Xerusian spacecraft. Mithra issued customization orders before he left to intercept Xenith. Smart move. It's all the scarlet-eyed creature needs to capitulate. His minions nod their heads, excitingly. Star Pyron will provide fuel for a very long time. The aids back away from Vane, providing an unobstructed view of his reaction to the proposition.

You present an irresistible offer, Mithra. I agree to call off the seize in exchange for these vast coffers of fuel. This more than adequate supply will allow Xerus and Reji to maintain peace within our realms. Jericho, send the message to abort the seize in Helenox.

Mithra lets the Xerusian leader think he has gotten the best end of the deal. This race will eventually die, like so many others Reji have dealt with in the past. Races who have no belief in an afterlife. However, Vane must be monitored for compliance. He cannot be trusted.

Chapter Eighteen-Your Place or Mine

Nick pulls the door open. Olivia smiles at him, looking hot as hell, but a little tired. Freshly changed from her flight suit into a pair of comfortable grey sweats and an off-the-shoulder, lavender sweatshirt. They had separated earlier to attend different meetings after strenuous low-Mars orbit training in reusable rockets manufactured by engineers from a joint JAXA/NASA project. Things have been progressing quickly over the last few weeks.

IVOSS's rocket development department is moving toward a test launch of a much more powerful prototype into the red planet's thin atmosphere. Both astronauts have thousands of hours under their belts in space aeronautic training through the US Naval Academy and NASA. Next month, they will join three others to engage in landing operations using low-slung crew modules which position themselves quite close to the planetary surface. Technology and development have been exploding with no indication of slowing down.

Nick grabs one delicate hand, pulling her close and shuts the door. As usual, she smells divine.

I really care about this woman. She's not only beautiful but smart as hell, too. We're both exactly where we need to be. With each other.

"Doing okay?" Nick's dark brows furrow with concern. "You were sort of quiet up there, this afternoon."

Olivia hasn't been asked that in what seems like forever. Most other guys she previously dated cared only about themselves. She remembers the news she has been withholding from him.

Should I tell him yet? Olivia hides her apprehension.

"Just a little blahh."

Maybe later. I need his body right now.

"I've been wanting to see more of your place." Olivia's eyes lock on Nick's for a few seconds, followed by a long look over his shoulder, down the hallway.

A soft light is coming out of the room, and she can hear faint music. It draws her like a magnet.

That has to be your bedroom. Show it to me, Nick. And don't stop there..

Nick's eyes watch as Olivia twirls the drawstring of her pants, teasing him by taking her time. His voice drops to a deep, sexy level, and he responds after reading her mind, perfectly.

"Would you like to step into my boudoir? It's very plain. I usually come to your place, but this is a nice change, even if my decorating skills suck. I do have other skills, though." Nick arches his left brow, making her weak in the knees.

When Olivia enters the bedroom, she's impressed by how neat it is. A light blanket and top sheet are folded down, as if he's had the bed prepared all day, just for her. Two glasses of dandelion wine rest invitingly on the nightstand. A single candle burns in a votive glass between them.

Mmmm-vanilla. How did he know that's my favorite?

Other than the candle, the only other light comes from a holomon television. Its screensaver is set to burning logs on a fire. Familiar music plays from a sound bar.

"Is that the score from *Dr. Zhivago*?" Olivia asks. "I recognize "Somewhere My Love."-a timeless piece."

"It is. My parents loved classical and so do I. Along with country and a lot of rock. You?"

"I can listen to just about anything. This song is beautiful." Olivia turns to face Nick, rises up on her toes and kisses his mouth tenderly. Stepping back, she slowly lifts the sweatshirt off. Braless. Nick's breathing quickens, his dark eyes drinking in her gorgeous body. Next, the pants are rolled down to step out of. She's only wearing one thing now.

"Crotchless panties? Fucking sweet."

Nick watches her lay back on queen-size pillows, nipples hard and ready for lovemaking. She lifts long, smooth legs onto the bed, looking at him hungrily. Green irises flash golden specks in the light from the candle. With one hand she begins to arouse herself. "Get over here."

Nick moves to the side of the bed. He lifts his shirt over his head, revealing washboard abs and just enough chest hair to feel incredibly enticing in her feverish hands. She gently massages his firm pecs and then slides soft hands downward, easing his sweatpants off.

"Jesus, you're ready for me," Olivia gasps.

She pulls off the Calvin Klein briefs, never taking her eyes off Nick's. His engorged manhood springs out. She teases it with her tongue, starting slowly and working her way up, flitting the tip like a Cobra snake. His moaning excites her more.

"That feels so good. Keep going, Liv." Nick's raspy voice urges her sucking. Up, down, and all around. His passion rises to a crescendo until he explodes, pulling long bunches of her hair back with just the right amount of force, his groin pulsating from sweet orgasm. After he's spent himself, they fall back onto the bed, breathing heavily.

"Damn, you sure know how to please a man." Nick's ragged breath is broken by an appreciative sigh. Olivia hands him his glass of wine and grabs her own. Their glasses clink together. The wine tastes wonderful. Just like their lovemaking.

"You sure know how to flatter a girl." She bats her eyelashes at him and giggles softly. "Ready to watch something?"

Nick voice commands the holomon to pull up old blockbuster movies. "Pick one, Liv. You don't mind if I call you that, I hope?" One finger plays with a tendril of her hair.

"Not at all. Especially when we're fucking. How about that one?"

Nick stops on Titanic, rolls his eyes and laughs. "Play."

The two lovebirds are ravenous, so they pause the movie after a few minutes. Nick orders in a dinner of chicken wings, cold slaw and a couple pieces of apple pie. It doesn't take long before an android stands outside the door, waiting for the delivery notification to reach Nick.

After receiving notice on his wrist device, he dresses and walks to the door to take a quick look through the peephole before opening it. A robot stands in the hallway, wearing a dark blue shirt, black pants, and highly polished black shoes. Its face is expressionless. A silver nametag with the name "ACharles-1010", the "A" standing for android, gleams under the harsh LED lights. In its right, incredibly humanlike hand, a to-go bag hangs at hip level under a white-knuckled grip. The left arm hangs limply by his side, palm facing inward, fingers motionless.

"Good evening, Mr. Johansen. Here is the order you placed."

ACharles presents the bag to Nick with a stiff arm, now sporting a plastered, white smile on its wrinkleless face. The kind of smile only a robot can show. Rather forced and overly sustained, like the smile a funeral director flashes during selection of a deceased's coffin, pallid hands gesturing toward expensive mahogany behemoths. Programmers have not been able to master natural human expressions and mannerisms. There's still a long way to go with facial transplants over electronic parts.

Nick takes the items, says thanks, and watches the robot walk away, feeling slightly creeped out. Most humans make small, unconscious moves with their heads when they walk, like glancing to the side or at their feet. The android's head remains rigidly fixed straight ahead as he proceeds down the long hallway. His body looks like something that would fit in on a Ford assembly line. Mechanical and precise. Nick watches until ACharles-1010 turns the corner.

I'm never going to feel comfortable around those fuckers. Especially one on one situations.

Back inside, he brings the food into the bedroom, grabbing a tray from underneath the bed.

"That dude, I mean robot, kind of freaks me out." Nick says between mouths of coated wings. "I've tried to be more relaxed around them, but I can't seem to get there entirely. Maybe it's because of the dumbass human names, hard to stomach when everyone knows they are not human at all. IVOSS should change that."

"I feel the same way. They make me uneasy, too. Shit, *my* stomach feels queasy all of a sudden, Nick. I'm sorry."

Fuck my life. Why now?

Olivia jumps up and runs to the bathroom. The wings and slaw come back up violently. Nick comes in to gently hold her cascading hair back while she wretches, telling her she'll be okay.

She takes a wet washcloth from him, holding it on her forehead and weakly rises to sit on the commode. Nick flushes the nastiness away. All he wants to do is protect this woman.

"Oh, Liv, I'm so sorry. Did the wings upset your stomach?"

"A little. Do you have any mouthwash? I'm feeling better now." Olivia takes the Dixie cup and rinses the bad taste out of her mouth. She decides it's now or never.

"Nick, I've been afraid to tell you. I was a few days late on my period, so I took a pregnancy test this morning. It came back positive."

Chapter Nineteen-Situations Change Rapidly

Nick's reaction to Olivia's statement is a blank stare. She puts a trembling hand over her mouth, crying softly. After a few seconds, initial shock on his face is replaced by a boyish grin.

"Are you sure, Liv? This is wonderful news!" Nick helps Olivia stand, drapes a cotton robe over her sobbing shoulders and lifts her up in his arms. She can smell his masculine scent. Breathing it in relaxes unsteady emotions.

"You're not angry with me? I have to admit something." She looks up at Nick through long, wet eyelashes. "I was less than diligent with birth control. It hasn't been a priority to keep up with. Something made me nonchalant about it. I feel horrible but I need to be completely honest with you. Are you terribly angry with me?"

"Hell no! We're going to have a child together! I've wanted to be a father for a long time." Nick's eyes exude excitement and love for the woman of his dreams. Olivia is going to give him something precious. A baby! He sets her down and lowers himself to one knee. Taking both her hands in his Nick looks into her beautiful emerald eyes.

"Liv, will you marry me?" his voice is soft but full of emotion. "We can get a ring later, babe."

Olivia has an angelic glow. The apples of her soft cheeks are pink and warm, as if she's been standing close to a blazing fire.

Is this the man I want to spend the rest of my life with?

It only takes a few seconds to realize that Mr. Right has been right next to her for a while now. The fact that he is so quick to propose, even after a nausea attack and ensuing pregnancy confession, shows how deeply he cares.

"Yes, Nick, yes! I would love to be your wife!" Olivia's sad sniffles turn to happy tears.

"Let's tell the housing department to find us a family unit." Nick is excited at the prospect of sharing a place together.

The two astronauts embrace. Little do they know the child Olivia carries does not belong to Nick.

For Dr. Susan Dorfmeyer, events leading up to her taking a pregnancy test don't transpire the same way as Olivia's, yet they're every bit as compelling.

Patient appointments in the medical clinic are repeatedly interrupted by frantic trips to the restroom. Her nausea isn't letting up one bit. Today was rough. She fights through it, immersing herself in the care of others. After the workday ends, the doctor impulsively has a blood draw performed by an AI device. Her reasoning is that it will help rule out the nagging suspicions in her head.

I'll review the hCG test results remotely. Maybe order some soup and crackers when my appetite comes back. This nausea shit is getting old, fast.

A hot belch comes up. She manages to swallow it down before stepping in to see her next patient.

I'm ready for this shift to end. At least all the patients are doing well. That makes me feel a little better.

A long nap after work improves her queasiness. Rising for a drink, she stops to gaze out her window at the velvet-black, Martian night. It looks peaceful, almost like an extremely remote location on Earth.

But this isn't Earth. This is Mars and I need to face reality.

She takes a deep breath calming her racing heart before accessing the lab results via a wrist device.

Here goes nothing.

Vivid blue eyes reflect shock. Even though she instinctively knew ahead of time what the report would show, it's a punch in the gut. She swallows and fights back tears.

Positive. What the hell. Gary and I made love the night before I left. I'm sure he didn't pull out, but he's had a vasectomy, for Christ's sake! How is this fucking possible?

Susan frowns. *Good job. Blame everyone but yourself. Guess I fall into the one percent of the female population who can still conceive after a man undergoes a vasectomy procedure. I should be ashamed of myself. There are many patients who would love to switch places with me.*

The doctor laughs ironically as the shock gradually wears off. She unconsciously puts a hand over her stomach.

*I have a PhD in how to help others with their reproductive issues, yet I ignored telltale signs from my own body that **I'm** impregnated. Late on my period, constantly nauseous, and my boobs are so goddamn sore. Fuck.*

The doctor massages her aching breasts while she thinks things through. She and Gary had decided two children were enough. Now what is she going to do? Will her position at the clinic become compromised?

I'll talk to Dr. Balabanov in the morning. Let him and the rest of the staff know right away.

The situation doesn't have to be looked upon as critical. Maybe, just maybe, Gary will understand that the duration of her mission has become even more uncertain. He's been so wonderful, putting his teaching career on hold to oversee the kids. Remote tutoring jobs have sufficed but Susan knows he misses in-person interaction with students. Will this tear their marriage apart? She prays he'll understand.

The following day, Dr. B, which he prefers to be called, congratulates her on the good news. Three obstetric nurse practitioners deliver all babies on the colony with great outcomes. Only two newborns have suffered severe illness. Luckily, both recovered fully. Nurse practitioners in the United States are now allowed to provide comprehensive labor and delivery care, dating back to the year 2050. They continue to showcase knowledge and skill, having overcome widespread skepticism in record time.

Mars was the natural place to continue practicing groundbreaking medicine in a neo-environment. After receiving extensive space travel training in the states, the NP providers prepared for a commercial rocket journey eager to embrace unexplored frontiers. Dr. Dorfmeyer will be in good hands when the time comes, both professionally and personally.

She records a teary-eyed video to Gary and the kids after work. It takes an hour to build up the courage. Hitting send on the recorded message means there is no turning back or returning to Earth anytime soon.

Just do it. Send the damn thing. That's all you have to do.

"Message sent." A monotone voice confirms transmission.

There, it's done. Susan climbs into bed, full of renewed determination. Her head turns to the window in time to observe a faint streak of light racing across the sky. A shooting star. She takes it as a good omen.

It's a sign, for sure. She strokes her stomach, absentmindedly. *Our place is here, no matter what Gary and the kids say.*

Doctor Dorfmeyer's head grows heavy. A hardcover book slips from limp hands. Her chin falls as she dreamily recalls a life altering event that recently occurred aboard an alien vessel amidst the stars. Fitzgerald's, *The Great Gatsby*, drops to the floor, landing with a soft thud. She hears someone speaking.

Am I awake or asleep? That voice, it's fading away....

Susan dozes. Mithra's words fill her head, urging her to do that which has never been done before. She jerks awake and sleepily looks at the novel on the floor. Its pages turn as if blown by warm breaths, until they lazily fall entirely to the left, floating down like the burnt ashes of a campfire. The haunting passage comes into view: "So we beat on, boats against the current, borne back ceaselessly into the past."

Deliver this child of our coupling, human, and your soul will be transported to a ***future*** *which never ends.*

Susan sleeps while Mithra's deep, soothing voice penetrates her dreams, easing any trepidation she formerly felt and replacing it with euphoric expectation.

IVOSS will record another healthy childbirth. Her family on Earth will soon lose precedence. The seed of a Reji alien grows not only within her womb—it metastasizes to her brain, supercharging maternal instincts to further protect the hybrid offspring.

Rest, beautiful human. Let your body recall how you felt when we joined together.

The doctor twitches and murmurs while she sleeps, as only a woman can, when she surrenders to phantom beings or oftentimes complete strangers that titillate and tease during imagined sexual rendezvous. These are wonderful, fantastical dreams. Oftentimes, elicited orgasms resulting from mental arousal are more intense than those derived from physical touch. Such is the power of the human mind. Mithra knows this. He has coupled with other alien species who feel nothing. Humans are quite sensitive to their desires.

Earthling, I will guide you from this night forward. Let the fruit of our coupling grow. You will soon hold a child for whom you will do anything. When you awaken the way will be clear.

Chapter Twenty-Visions

Olivia's eyes flutter open. It's the middle of the night. Nick lies next to her in bed where they made love four hours ago. She can hear his smooth, relaxed breathing and gently touches his hard, muscular back.

I must have worn him out. Damn, what a lover. And he's so tender afterward. How did I get this lucky? It's also a little chilly in here. Wait, am I dreaming?

Covers kicked down on her side. Cold feet. Sitting up halfway, she realizes the light has been sucked out of the room. Groggy eyes try to adapt but it's like being enclosed in a coffin. Everyone's worst nightmare.

It's pitch black in here. Frigid hands slide down her hips.

W*hat the hell? I thought I put my panties back on before we called it a night but—shit! I'm stark naked and damn, so fucking aroused!* Rubbing swollen breasts.

My nipples are like knife points and my groin is aching. Jesus. Olivia falls back onto the pillow, raising slim arms over her head. *I wish Nick would wake up and tie my hands to the headboard. I'd let him fuck me again, right now. Whomever said pregnancy sex is some of the best you can have, was right on.*

Suddenly, as she turns to stroke her bed partner awake, her hand stops in midair, fingers tingling slightly, as if she had lain on them for too long, impeding the blood flow to the tips. The sensation moves slowly up her arm. She senses a foreign entity in the space around her. Gossamer thin memories from the prior alien encounter hang where they are at least slightly retrievable. Mithra's sonorous voice fills her head.

Earthling-allow me to enter your mind while your physical self enjoys the release it requires. It is I, Mithra. Leader of the Reji race. Ruler of The Reborn. Keeper of Knowledge. Master of Minds. Prophet of The Syren. I am all these things combined. And I offer you more than sexual satisfaction. I offer an afterlife. Listen to my words....

Olivia's body jerks as Mithra speaks to her mind. Although highly curious what is happening, she feels no fear.

Human, I seek your desire to join with me again. To experience what you now know to be true. Do you wish to be a part of this utopian destination? If you choose to join me, you can live....forever. You will make a mind-altering transition to the afterlife humans desperately desire. I am here to tell you one exists. Within the Syren.

Olivia is now able to discern Mithra's prone form hanging over her highly aroused body. This time however, she has questions for him and is able to reign in her sexual longing. He listens closely. Her intense inquisitiveness moves him in a way he has seldom experienced.

Mithra, I'm confused. What do you mean when you say forever? With whom can I share this supposed utopian existence? You? Your alien race? You mean nothing to me, other than providing sexual release and a brief glimpse of what you profess to be true. And why have you selected **me** *for this "intervention"?*

Present to me the assurance that I will be rejoined with those humans in my life circle who meant something to me while I was alive on Earth. Without this foundation of love, mankind has nothing, for only love provides an impetus to join your exodus. I have lost a dear brother who idolized me. Will I ever be with him again?

Olivia begins to cry. She misses her little brother, more than ever.

I wish I could communicate with my voice and not just my mind. I want to tell Shiloh how far we have progressed in space exploration.

Suddenly, she feels soft kicks within her abdomen. At five months along in her pregnancy, the timing is normal. She has no idea the child is only half hers. She's about to learn the truth.

Relax, earthling. Your body bears the fruits of our coupling. Do not be upset. I will guide your human consciousness into "unchartered waters", a human euphemism often voiced, yet poorly understood. Your loved ones will be reunited with you ***if*** *you agree to raise the offspring we have created to maturity. Join us, Olivia.*

What? Are you insane? Olivia gradually absorbs Mithra's words, like a child learning the letters of the alphabet or how to grasp an object. The weight of his words is unbelievably hard to accept.

Reji seek to share that which we experience ourselves. The Syren, an entity older than time itself, where our race was spawned, grants us power beyond human understanding. We were instructed to locate other species to couple with so that they may enjoy comparable abilities. The human race appears ripe for outside assistance. Mankind is eager to know for sure that ***life exists after death of bodily functions.*** *Your male counterpart's brain was taken shortly after your arrival on this red planet. Reji needed to analyze it. His conscious memory has been uploaded to the Syren where it will exist, forever.*

Are you for real? What the fuck are you filling my mind with? The baby is Nick's. Not yours! Olivia feels sick to her stomach. Nick will be devastated. It's all lies! She tries to move to shake him awake but her limbs won't budge.

How does she know what this alien says is true? Can she really be united with Shiloh in some way, shape, or form? Hot tears pour out of her eyes. This mental conversation is getting way over her head, while at the same time, filling her broken heart over the loss of her little brother with hope. Hope, another emotion mankind uses to keep going in the face of despair. Mithra wipes her tears away, his touch incredibly soft and warm.

Star Rejenitus constantly fuels our existence and those we bring into our fold. I realize this information is very difficult to accept as truth. The Syren is a cosmic utopia which surrounds the Luxar Galaxy. It spawns new stars which eventually merge with ours. Our race wishes for others to realize that immortality ***can*** *be achieved if you allow infiltration of our alien race into your DNA. Let me lead you. The process will be gradual at first. Come with me. You have but* ***one*** *chance to participate. Reji are not allowed to offer this opportunity more than once. We are extremely selective of those races we choose. Look, now, at what mankind's future can hold...*

Once again, an exquisite mind fuck plays out, courtesy of Mithra's injected mental imagery. He shows images of Shiloh urging her to accept what is asked of her. Afterward, Olivia is exhausted but ecstatic. She will do anything to be with her brother again. The initial shock of learning Nick is not the father of the baby fades like smoke from a blown-out candle. Her path has been chosen. Only hell with keep her from its destination.

Chapter Twenty-One-Breakup

"What the hell, Nicole. Are you fucking kidding me?" Devon McDonald is boiling inside. After watching her breakup video message he's wasting no time recording a heated reply.

Per his now ex-fiancé, she stated that someone new has captured her heart. She didn't mean for it to happen, but it was 'inevitable', pointing out that Devon seemed to be more fired up about the Mars mission than making plans for their wedding, even if it was far out on her never-ending social calendar. Nicole even returned the engagement ring he had painstakingly picked, placing it into his mom's reluctantly outstretched hand, during a confession-filled lunch date. The crocodile tears were probably falling in full force.

Mom must be heartbroken, too. Goddamn you, Nicole.

"I told you it would be hard to provide input on wedding plans until I return." Devon glares at the lens. "You apparently lied to my face when you said that was okay."

Fuck you and the white horse your Prince Prick rode in on. Enjoy the fashion fuckfest. That's what Devon wants to say. Instead, he takes a deep breath before cutting ties with the woman he thought would be there for him. A hard lesson learned.

"Do whatever makes you happy, Nicole. I'm sorry you decided I'm not worth waiting for. I won't contact you again." Devon sends the reply message. He could spit. Spit the bitter taste of rejection onto the floor. Instead, he walks to the kitchen and opens the small freezer.

I need a goddamn drink. Fuck it. Good riddance. Now, I can really focus on the mission the way I want to. I'll tell mom to sell the ring. Her and dad can use the money for that hot tub they've been wanting.

Top shelf Jose Cuervo tequila over ice with a lime chaser can cure a lot of things. A small bottle rests in the freezer, beckoning to him like a Vegas prostitute. The liquor slowly heats his stomach, burning into frazzled nerves. Two more shots induce a "whatever" feeling. Tomorrow is a new day. He's not going to let Nicole ruin another one.

A public announcement interrupts his shower the following morning. Devon shuts the water off via voice command, opens the door and grabs a towel to dry off. Coming from a long line of physically fit McDonalds, he's nothing short of a stud. There isn't an ounce of fat on his hard, shredded body. He's blessed with the kind of physique one could look at a for a very long time, if only in appreciation of God-given attributes.

Devon could easily garner a loyal following of ardent fans on the newest app craze on Earth, Vidbidz. Subscribers bid on sole rights to videos of the hottest bodies on the planet, dropping tokens like hotcakes in order to become top fans along with a chance to meet the subjects in person via highly anticipated drawings. People will pay for just about anything. Sex sells and always will.

"Good morning. This is President Peters with a colony-wide public service announcement. An investigation was recently concluded in regard to the sudden death of one of our maintenance technicians. This incident occurred during the record-breaking dust storm while attempting to repair a rover. Final autopsy results indicated he had an unexpected stroke which led to his collapse and unfortunate passing. An extended memorial in Everett Pickens' honor will remain on display for the rest of the week inside Building 102C."

Devon pauses in mid-stride toward his apartment door, his improved mood suddenly soured.

Funny how he's leaving out the rest of what fucking happened. Those asshats think we were seeing things. Why are they trying to cover up events leading to Everett's death? They must know something we don't. He reaches for the door handle but stops to hear any last words from the colony's president.

"I want to express my continued gratitude for the hard work that is carried out daily on IVOSS. Each and every one of you plays a vital part in the colony's future. Keep it up."

Jesus, I can't wait to talk to the others at breakfast. Do they think we experienced shared psychosis disorder?

Devon is so lost in thought when he walks out the door, he fails to see Veronica approaching.

"Hey, you," V greets him with a gorgeous smile. It lights up her face and his mood. She has her long, jet-black hair pulled back. Devon thinks she's incredibly hot, made more so by the smart stuff between those small, delicate ears. Star-shaped, silver stud earrings provide the perfect complement to dark features. He feels that same sensation as before. A pleasant warmth in his groin. It makes him want to retreat inside with his mouth on her full, rosy lips.

Damn, I'd like to get to know this girl behind closed doors. She makes me feel so good inside. I can't help it. He returns her smile.

"Hey, yourself V! Did you hear that PA? Who does Peters think he's fooling?"

"No shit! I saw the ship better than anyone. It wasn't some half-assed viewing from miles away. It was up close and personal. I could **feel** something giving me the once-over. I'll always feel guilty about it, Devon. Why did they leave me alone?"

"Man, I'm sorry, V." Devon touches her shoulder lightly. He wants to comfort her. The attraction is shared. She actually leans into it, unconsciously. Something magnetic exists between them.

Quantum One's crew sits with Mike and the Skyport Transfer team in a packed Starlight Diner. They've just heard the announcement. Olivia is hot. Her green eyes could cut rock. The president's lack of information is ridiculously misleading.

"You guys, I know you're used to seeing me fairly cool-headed—but that dumbfuck Peters is covering something up. They debriefed each of us for about ten minutes and that was it. Hush, hush. Are they that afraid of the truth?" Nick reaches for her hand. Since becoming a couple, they've restrained from being too touchy around the others. It's not their thing.

Dr. Dorfmeyer is in shock. What the hell is happening? Didn't Dr. Lee tell the president about the unexplained autopsy findings? She's not happy, either. Why are crucial details being withheld from the public? IVOSS is supposed to be a completely transparent community. Susan drops her voice down. The others lean in to hear her speak.

"He sure didn't mention a damn thing about that alien ship. The colony needs to be on high alert! For God's sake, I stood next to Dr. Lee during Everett's autopsy. His brain was anatomically altered. Two lobes were gone." It grows silent at the table, a cloud of doom settling in as if they now sit in a deserted, fog-enshrouded outdoor café in the heart of Soho.

"Are you serious?" Nick feels like things are getting increasingly weird around IVOSS. He vows to stay even more alert.

Olivia presses a button. A hole opens in the center of the table. Dirty dishes and utensils move toward it on the now-mobile table surface; they fall silently like a world-class cliff diver competing at Serpent's Lair in Ireland. The disposal chute leads to lower-level recycling processes.

"I think we should request a group meeting with him and his little minion, Hamilton." Olivia suggests the idea emphatically. "Maybe even go over his head."

"You do that, and we're fucked," Mike says. "They'll ship us home so fast our heads will spin. I don't know about you guys, but Earth is the last place I want to be. There's nothing left for me there. I came here to be a part of something big. If it includes dealing with aliens, so be it."

"Speak for yourself," Janice pipes up. "I want to keep my entire brain, thank you." She shudders. Mike rolls his eyes.

"Still, a group meeting with the brass might clarify if the ship sighting has been hushed up. I'll let you know what comes of my request. Stay alert peeps."

Chapter 22-A New Breed

Nothing ever comes of Olivia's request for a meeting with the colony's president. Everett Pickens' remains, along with the crew's reports of an alien spacecraft, are catapulted into space like nomad satellites searching for non-existent signals. As the days and months go on, Q-One's crew immerse themselves in work, increasingly acceptive of the fact that the occurrence was brushed under the proverbial regolith rug. But not everything remains below the surface. Some signs are becoming noticeable on ground level.

Time diffuses all seemingly critical situations for most life forms, particularly if you've been heavily influenced to move on, as in the cases of Dr. Dorfmeyer and Commander Newman. The surrogates shift their focus to the future and what waits inside their growing wombs. An alien strain of DNA infiltrates hybrid fetuses, merging with human cells to create a baseline of Reji mitochondria. Upon maturity, this DNA will evolve to be almost entirely that of a Reji, although remnants of human DNA will remain for outward appearances. Genius.

In the same manner Reji spacecraft cloak themselves in obscurity, so too, Reji offspring will cloak their bodies, assuming an outward human semblance, when necessary. Yet, their reasons for taking control are not based on hostility, but rather divine intent. Reji seek to instill a desire for human inclusion in something they have been aware of for eons.

Immortality. Existing in its purest form. Consciousness. 'I think, therefore I am.' Aptly deciphered by Descartes, the great French philosopher. From thoughts spring eternal life.

My pregnancy has flown by. Susan muses while doing low impact exercises. *Shit, I have to pee, again.* Pressure on her bladder creates a constant urge. She drops down to sit on the commode.

Gary and the kids were less than thrilled when I told them, months ago. He knows the baby can't be his. They haven't contacted me since. Fine, I have every-

thing I need right here. They can travel to see me. Right-like ***that*** *will ever happen.* A hollow laugh hangs in the air. *Wow, it's almost like I'm a completely different person now.* More sardonic laughter. *So be it.*

Dr. Dorfmeyer's interest in her current family lessens each day. It's not that she doesn't love them; it's more of a preoccupation with the here and now coupled with recognition of what she has been chosen to do. Returning to the living room of her apartment, she voice commands her holomon to load 3-D images of the baby, taken at the clinic earlier by an expert sonographer. It instantly displays a series of pictures, showing length, weight and all the gestational data an expectant mom could ask for. It's a girl and she has already positioned herself to be born in the next few days. Susan is obsessed.

Happy tears fall onto a Disney-patterned maternity top as she enters the nursery. Motion-activated lullabies softly fill the air, encircling and serenading her in an almost trancelike manner. Worries about the family are left behind. Lowering a top-heavy body down to the glider gel-back rocker, a few hard kicks can be discerned through the fabric of her top. She grins, absentmindedly stroking her swollen stomach.

I'm ready to hold you, Cassiopeia. My little Cassi. Whispering endearments, eyes glassy. *Mama loves you. Get here, baby girl.*

Not far from Dr. Dorfmeyer's apartment, the couples and family quarters have had a slight increase in births. Although marriage is not required on the Mars outpost, both parental parties must sign a legal agreement in which they testify to care for their children, be they of natural birth or adoption. Thus far, no children have been placed in the care of adoptive parents; the steps to follow, if requested, are in place, should that scenario arise.

Nick, freshly showered and stark naked, walks behind Olivia who is making a cup of coffee. He presses up against her backside releasing cascades of honey-toned hair. It's so thick and beautiful, he can't resist burying his face in it, relishing the faint floral fragrance of Herbal Essence shampoo.

"Nick, I told you, I can't have sex right now. I'm too close to delivery. Damn, you are a horny man." Olivia throws back her head, giggling.

Since becoming impregnated, he constantly reminds Olivia how attractive she is. She leans into him, crossing toned arms loosely over herself in a half-hearted attempt to avoid his wandering hands and rock-hard member. Irresistible temptation threatens to delay her obstetric visit.

"Liv, you just look so damn hot, all the fucking time." Nick reaches around her enlarged stomach, sliding warm hands under the tight maternity top. "How's our baby boy?" They had learned the sex months ago, both agreeing they wanted to know ahead of time. He kisses the area where the baby is kicking, making mom laugh.

Olivia's engorged nipples leak a small amount of milk. Nick starts to pull and twirl them in just the right way, causing more aroused leakage.

"Mmmm, Nick Johansen, stop, you're making my boobs leak too much." She steps to the side, swiping the drips away while turning to kiss Nick's nose.

"Get dressed, ya animal." We have an NP visit in twenty minutes. "I'm so excited to deliver our baby!" She pushes the father-to-be into the bedroom. "Hurry up, or we'll be late." Nick turns at her command, mimicking a Chippendale stripper for good measure.

Olivia feels pangs of guilt at her deception. The father of this child is not human, yet she cannot stop the progression of something so remarkable, so unbelievable, that, somehow, she *does* believe it. Her destiny has been forged. Looking down at her swollen stomach, she feels more sharp kicks. The feeling erases the guilt, filling her with excitement.

"I love you baby boy. We can't wait to meet you."

OB/GYN team lead, Melody Shotts, NP, loves her position on the IVOSS colony. Bringing new life into the world fills her with hope for the future of colonization. Each little baby will eventually contribute to the exploration of the universe. Isn't that one of the reasons mankind was created?

Two excited expectant parents, per a message on her wrist device, are ready to be seen in exam room 102. Melody walks toward it from the central nursing station in the ward. She enjoys pumping up her ancillary staff with compliments and frequently brings treats, like doughnuts and chocolates. Good thing a workout area is next to the maternity ward.

Inside Room 102, Nick and Olivia greet her as she walks in. The excitement on both their faces is evident.

"Good morning! I've already reserved our biggest and best labor/delivery room! Anything new I should know about?"

"Yes," Nick quips with a twinkle in his eye. "I can't get her to stop eating everything in sight. She's a vacuum cleaner!"

Melody laughs and watches Olivia playfully punch Nick's arm.

"Yes!" My water broke on the way here! The contractions have been mild, though, ever since."

Nick helps her lie back on the exam table. She's ecstatic because everything seems to be falling into place for her and the man she hopes to spend the rest of her life with. In fact, two months ago, they were married in a short but sweet ceremony that only included Quantum One's crew members. A larger wedding will be held back home but that can wait.

"Wow," Melody remarks. Her gloved hands check to see how far along things are progressing. "You are fifty percent effaced and dilated to almost 4cm! I think you should be admitted!

"Really? That's wonderful!" Olivia kisses her assistant commander at the good news.

"Hell, yeah!" Nick does a little fist pump, helping his wife back to a sitting position.

"Our bags are packed. We'll contact the RTD department to let them know we won't be coming in this morning, or, for that matter, a few months!" Both parents on IVOSS receive six months of parental leave after the birth of a child.

"Great guys! I'm starting my rounds. The labor nurses will get you checked in and comfortable. See you in a couple hours. By the way, I love the name you picked out for the baby boy-Remus Matthew Johansen. I bet he is destined for quite a future!"

Chapter 23-Watch Me Now

Veronica can't get Devon off her mind. Here of late, the two have been running into each other in the refreshment center of their housing unit. She sees him approaching and can't help but feel like he's doing it on purpose.

Fine with me. I know he's not a fucking perv like some other idiots I've dated. In fact, there's not much I don't like about this guy. He's sweet, crazy smart, and damn, that body....

"Hey-what's up?" Devon smiles, making Olivia weak in the knees, which hasn't happened for quite a long time. "We seem to be seeing each other a lot down here."

What the hell, girl. Go for it.

"Devon! Hey yourself. Just grabbing a little something to unwind. Busy day. You?"

"Same."

Do it. Ask him to come over.

"Ummm." She looks at him shyly. "Would you like to join me for dinner in about an hour? I can air fry salmon steaks and add a side of fresh-picked petite potatoes with French-cut green beans. The only thing I don't have is dessert." Her hint is obvious.

Long pause. Two sets of dark eyes lock in. Soaking up good vibes and good intentions.

"That sounds delicious. I'll bring a bottle of wine." The smile never leaves his face, but she detects something else in his hazel eyes.

V controls the urge to bring a hand up to rub the Martian five o'clock shadow on the engineer's chiseled jaw. She concentrates on preparing Celestial vanilla tea. A stray strand of jet-black hair falls over downcast eyes.

"Hold on. You're coming undone." Warm fingers gently place the wayward lock behind her ear intentionally brushing her soft cheek. Seconds click off the wall-mounted clock in the atrium. V is sure she is blushing.

"Thanks." She returns his smile and heads to the elevator. "See you soon."

Later, they enjoy dinner and a movie, talking about where life has taken them thus far and all the lessons they've learned along the way.

"Want to go for a walk?" Devon suggests. "The new Opis Observatory is almost complete, and it has kickass reclining seats. I know it's late but I'm the restless type. Sometimes, I have a little trouble falling asleep and will take walks around the colony to loosen up. Usually, the only ones still awake are the droids. I'm still getting used to those fuckers."

Veronica giggles. "No shit-they give me the creeps, too. I don't feel entirely comfortable around them. I've been wanting to check out the observatory, too. Let me grab my shoes." V opens the hall closet, bending over to grab a pair of Nikes.

Damn, that's a nice ass. I'd like to squeeze those sweet cheeks. A picture of an older woman on a bookcase catches Devon's eye, diverting horny thoughts. He picks it up, smiling.

"Who's this attractive lady? Let me guess. Is it your mom?"

"Bingo. Her name is Isla. I miss her terribly. She's my number one fan." V's eyes turn a little glassy. "Sometimes, I feel horrible guilt about leaving her behind on Earth, but she constantly pushes me to follow my dreams."

Devon nods his head in agreement. He also misses his parents and knows they are extremely disappointed about losing Nicole as a prospective daughter-in-law.

I can't be blamed for falling for a shallow, self-centered bitch. Time to move on.

They step into the hallway. It's really late. Eerily quiet. Overhead lighting is excessively bright and there are one or two flickering sporadically. Devon takes V's hand. She smiles.

Warm hands. Mmmmm. I know what that means.

"The building's atrium has charged Segways waiting. "Let's head over to the Skyport complex. I remember where the utility elevator is. It will take us up to the observation deck. It's not set to open for a couple of days, but I think I know a way to override the system."

V laughs. "Dude, you've got balls."

"You know it." Devon gives her a sly look. He's been hacking systems his entire life. Why stop now?

Segways were relaunched around twenty years ago with much improved features like on board cameras and all kinds of sensors. The machines hum quietly as they ride them across the colony, past the RTD and into Skyport Sector 5B. Two reusable rockets stand sentinel, their inner electronics protected by flaps of thick, titanium shields.

"See that grey set of panels in the back? That's the utility elevator. They head in that direction and park the personal vehicles in different charging docks. V looks at Devon.

"Dude, are you sure this is ok? We might get caught."

Devon chuckles. "Girl, where's the risk-taker in ya? No one is around to see us. I put a temporary hold on surveillance cameras. Come on."

He punches in override commands. The elevator doors, usually kept in a locked status, open invitingly. Interior lighting is softer at night to conserve power. They step in. V's heartbeat quickens. Devon makes her feel alive. She's loving it. *What the hell. Let's see where this leads.*

They step into the gorgeous observatory chamber. A ceiling made entirely of breakproof polycarbonate separates them from the stars. Three huge, high-powered telescopes sit on steel platforms.

"Damn! Those are sweet!" V squeals with delight. She follows Devon, who is sprinting up the steps to reach the top row of reclined seats. Each one is heated, contains charging ports and buttons which command the closest telescope.

"Fucking fly!" Devon's like a little boy, pressing buttons as if playing pinball in an old arcade. V smacks his hands.

"Devon! Stop, you're going to fuck something up!" She whispers scoldingly in his ear, grabbing his shoulder at the same time.

With a few last jabs, Devon plugs in the parameters for Earth. The telescope makes a series of adjustments. They recline their seats entirely and hold hands again.

A blue planet slowly comes into focus. Home. Or what used to be home. Endless eddies of white mist envelope her like the thin veil of a blushing bride. Deep blue oceans frame convoluted land masses where billions of citizens and trillions of thoughts exist. So far away, like an abstract painting rendered from an artist's brush. Swirling, changing. Lonely.

"It's beautiful." V whispers. "Devon, I want you to make love to me. Right here." She places his hot hand on her thumping heart.

He's right. Taking risks can pay off big.

Devon's own heart thumps harder. He leans over to kiss Veronica's moist lips, moving down to her neck. She helps him take off her shirt, revealing a black lace bra that is so incredibly sexy it makes him hard with anticipation. Devon kisses one breast while rubbing his hand over the nipple on the other. He releases the front clasp, takes both breasts in his hands and buries his face in them passionately.

"Goddamn you, V." Breathing quickly now. "You'd better stop me. I'm about ready to bust out of my pants."

"Let me help you with those." She peels Devon's pants off, taking his erection in her soft hand. Stroking and tasting him to maddening heights.

"Watch me strip down for you." V leans back in the seat and slowly slides her pants off, followed by a black lace thong. Demurely allowing Devon to lustfully stare at her beautiful body. Straddling his, she slowly lowers herself onto him, groaning with pleasure. Devon voices his own excitement. Faster, faster, their union builds in intensity until they both climax at the same time, Earth forgotten in the midst of mutual lust.

Chapter Twenty-Four-Xerusian Meltdown

Star Pyron's hydrogen reserves continue to plummet. Vane's fleets refuel daily at a breakneck pace. A tenuous truce, reached by the Xerusian leader and Mithra, is based on his assurance that the gifted supply will be inexhaustible. Unfortunately, waning coffers are on the brink of becoming spent cosmic Bunsen burners.

To make matters worse, Vane has not been delivering sufficient amounts of fuel to his dying home star, Amorpheus. Somehow, most Xerus still idolize him, believing false propaganda that he still searches for additional supplies on multitudinous missions. Although his critics are few, a small number of dissenters, having realized how dire their predicament is, have agreed to form a secret council behind his back. The seed of unrest is growing slowly but surely.

Jericho catches his crimson-eyed leader in between fruitless journeys, during Xenith's umpteenth refueling on Pyron. The mechanism supplying the vessel sputters occasionally, sounding like the Green Giant coughing up phlegm. Their telepathic minds converse.

Vane, it's obvious we were lied to by Mithra about the life expectancy of Star Pyron's reserves. This was supposed to be the deal so we could save Amorpheus. We haven't brought any supplies home for way too long. There are only so many stars that have accessible supplies of fuel.

Zericho is careful to keep his voice respectful, for he does not want to incite his hot-headed commander more than usual.

You are correct. Two wrinkles form on Vane's tumescent forehead. He doesn't have the quickest intellect. It fires in only one direction. Forward. What lurks behind is too often ignored. Nott, his Xerusian mate on Amorpheus, is a good example. She currently seeks comfort in the beds of more attentive suitors, taking advantage of Vane's prolonged absences. A female Xeru's desires can only be ignored for so long.

Aware of her indiscretions, Vane chooses self-satisfaction via couplings with any willing participant in the cosmos, caring naught, not to be mistaken for Nott, about growing rumors that his relationship is crumbling. It's the hunt that matters. Certainly not a mate at home, whom he grows tired of. His thoughts, and loins, are occupied elsewhere.

I propose a targeted mission for Xerus to enact revenge. Our ***dear*** *friend Mithra and his Reji minions won't see it coming.*

Vane watches the refueling of Xenith, which is taking longer than expected. At the halfway point, the hydrogen pyre snuffs out, as if an omnipotent ogre has reached down with two fingers to pinch the flames. Vane snorts from razor thin nostril slits, releasing two streams of rushing air onto his sidekick. Zericho's suspended body shoots ten feet away from the force. He returns beside his commander, instead of in front, hiding slight perturbance at being blown away.

Tell me your plan, Vane. I'm all ears. This is just a joke for Xerus. Their anatomical ears are barely visible, if at all.

Reconnaissance vessels have clandestinely followed Reji ships to a red planet in a galaxy named The Milky Way. An alien race recently migrated there. Vane pauses with a perplexed look in his bleeding eyes. *What a strange name for a galaxy. What is 'Milky' supposed to even mean?* He looks at Jericho for an explanation, but the warrior offers no help. He wishes his commander would stay on point.

I haven't the slightest idea, Vane. These newbie species come up with the stupidest names. Jericho offers a vaporous reply.

They call the red planet Mars. It is next to another blue planet called Earth that has billions of beings called humans. Earth is their home base. As we know, Rejis claim to be capable of achieving immortality, which is utterly preposterous. To make things worse, Mithra now endeavors to brainwash this particular race into thinking they can join the so-called 'afterlife'. Rubbish! He has already planted his Reji seed into two females. The hybrids are due to be delivered any day. Mithra plans on using them to convert the colony's residents, using unprecedented mind and DNA manipulation. How ***noble*** *of him. Well, we are going to make it difficult if not impossible. He will pay for stiffing us on fuel!*

I propose we spoil their mission in a big way by sending ships to annihilate this outpost. After that, we will take out the population on Earth. Spies learned they are quite susceptible to attack, having only been in existence a few hundred thousand years! Can you believe that? Their defenses on this outpost are practically non-existent. Vane snorts again. What a snob he is.

Jericho, who is almost as blood thirsty as Vane, nods his domed head in excitement.

Master of Amorpheus, you have my support in a planned attack. However, what about the citizens back home who are depending on your return with more fuel? Our beloved star will be dead soon. I fear Xerus' future is quite dire.

Zericho, the Milky Way Galaxy possesses its own star that we can use. First, we must rid ourselves of the human race and hybrids that exist on its orbiting planets. We can kill two objectives with one stone. Decimate mankind ***and*** *enjoy nuclear longevity. I've called a meeting in Xenith's command hub to develop a plan. The ship has milked the last drop of power from this pitiful pyre. Come, there is much to discuss.*

Xenith's Command Hub is gargantuan, taking up two thirds of the vessel. Doma and Mirt, along with Jericho, float around its periphery as Vane calls the meeting to order. The core of his Xerusian invasion force forms a large group of gullible attendees whose bloodthirst is reflected in huge, non-blinking eyes. The reflection off their cerise orbs can be seen on the massive hologram filling the center of the room.

Good evening loyal warriors! Vane raises his flowing arm appendages in a welcoming gesture to eager Xerus. They respond with barely contained fervor. *Greetings, Vane!*

I am beyond excited to present a mission which holds the promise of unbelievable outcomes! Behold planet Earth and Mars, located in The Milky Way Galaxy. These planets are within close proximity of our warp speed vessels.

Vane approaches the hologram. His alien digits manipulate images of Mars and the human colony on its surface.

Xeru spies recently broached facilities in the stealth of night. The occupants of this outpost are weakling humans, ripe for invasion. Their weaponry is rudimentary. We will begin by sabotaging robotic humanoids to mount an uprising in the near future. They must be overtaken before the hybrid offspring multiply quickly. Vane pauses, allowing his red-tinged form to ascend, while turning bloodshot orbs down over his troops below.

It ***is*** *true that humans possess armaments of more serious capability on their home planet, Earth, but once we sabotage the Mars outpost, we can attack the* *'hive.' After we annihilate the human race, additional troops can join us to thrive on the sun in this galaxy. It will be the most difficult takeover Xerus have ever attempted. Are you with me soldiers?*

Torrid veins stand out on Vane's forehead, growing to three times their normal size as his alien heartbeat throbs from excitement. He nods approval, watching liquified forms rise. They begin a precisely circular movement around the chamber, eventually twirling so quickly that sparks can be seen. Their voices respond in unison into Vane's throbbing brain.

Yes! We will annihilate hybrids and humans! The Milky Way Galaxy will be ours! All hail Vane! Long live Xerus!

Chapter Twenty-Five-The Hybrid Births

The euphoria Susan experiences after Cassiopeia's birth is life-altering. How could so much love be felt for another being? From day one the newborn's deep azure eyes reflect an intelligence far beyond her infantile age. Small hands reach up to touch the human surrogate's face, capable of transmitting deep emotion. An unbreakable bond immediately forms, consuming mother and child.

Unfortunately, Susan's husband Gary filed for divorce three months ago. He never accepted any possibility of the child being his own. Susan understands he feels betrayed. In his mind, since he had a vasectomy, her pregnancy obviously resulted from an extramarital affair. He rarely has the older children communicate. She still cares for James and Zoe, but the present situation takes precedence. A new child fills her days with love and pride. The older kids will be fine with their dad.

Dr. Dorfmeyer decides to resume seeing patients at the medical clinic, even though her maternity leave is still in effect. Cassi is such an easy baby to care for. She rarely cries, babbling from her front carrier while Susan goes from exam room to exam room. The patients love the interaction, of course.

"Oh my-she's so cute!" A woman being seen in follow-up, is smitten with the baby. "Looks like she loves time with Doctor Mom!" Cassi's eyes are bright and intelligent, as if she can understand the woman.

Possessing an off-the-chart IQ, it soon becomes obvious Cassi is a gifted child. In fact, the very first night she slept in the bassinet, Susan hears her murmuring sounds that are usually made by a toddler. She is the mother of a prodigy. At night, the doctor's dreams are filled with images of the child growing and becoming very special. Each morning, when Susan awakens, she remembers a little bit more about the alien rendezvous which set the course for where she and Cassi presently are, awaiting a much bigger day in store for the colony's future. The doctor's gradual transition is in the cosmic cards.

One day after Cassiopeia's birth, Melody Shotts, FNP, delivers Remus Matthew Johansen. She tells Nick and Olivia it was the easiest she's ever had the pleasure of attending. The first-time parents cradle a robust baby boy with long-lashed amber eyes and a head topped by chestnut-colored fuzz. IVOSS has three daycares, but most days they keep Remus with them, exploring countless wonders of the Martian outpost, delighting in their son's reactions to others and his unique surroundings. Like Cassi, the hybrid child shows signs of being extremely gifted.

"When he's five, he'll be allowed to wear a terrasuit and explore Mars with us! Man, I can't wait!" Nick sounds like a kid himself, bubbling over with excitement about the future. Olivia can't help but feel the same way. Never in her wildest dreams did she think she would have a child in a place other than Earth. Now, the reality of it has settled in and it's the new norm. She had relayed a video message to her parents a few months back, introducing Nick and explaining fate had brought them together. Shocked at first about Olivia's pregnancy, the one thing that matters the most is their daughter's happiness. When they see their adorable grandson in videos their hearts melt.

"Honey, dad and I can see this is exactly what you needed. I know since you lost your brother, it's been incredibly difficult. A family is a wonderful thing. Congratulations! Please kiss baby Remus for us. He is absolutely adorable! Your dad and I hope we can meet him and Nick in person, sweetheart. There was a segment on the evening news about real-time video capability coming down the pipeline. Communication will be so much better then. Stay as long as you need to, but please, keep in touch. We love you."

As the two hybrid children mature their parents notice signs of profound intelligence. They are able to verbalize first words at a very early age and exhibit advanced fine motor skills. Both absolutely love story time. It's not long before favorite books are recited, word for word. The two kids, extremely close since birth, play daily in the recreation center, tumbling and shouting like normal kids, even though they are anything but. Olivia, like Susan, gleans more and more from nightly dreams, completely recalling her encounters with Mithra and accepting the mission with eagerness. She feels no immediate need to enlighten Nick. She'll wait until the time is right.

Martian sols tick by, much like they do on Earth for the most part, but something on the red planet is quite different. Cassi and Remus are practically inseparable, like twins. Demonstrating an exceptional aptitude at STEM programs, they are chosen to co-instruct advanced courses, eager to spread knowledge. Sometimes, after class, when it's just the two of them, they talk prophetically about what tomorrow holds, instinctively realizing that change is coming.

"Cass, what do you think is up with us? I know we aren't like others our age. We definitely have qualities that seem to be evolutionary. Sometimes, when I sleep at night, I see visions of a burning sun. It calls to me, as if I'm supposed to be there, instead of living out my life on this small, red planet. Do you dream the same thing?"

"Remus, I do. All the time. Something huge is going to happen when we turn eighteen, which is right around the corner. Every night my dreams include strange looking beings like those aliens we see in movies. Except, they're not hostile at all. When I wake up, I can't remember much, but I've been writing down what I do recall, so I'll have a record of it. We're being groomed for a cataclysmic event. Something that will change mankind, forever." Cassi grabs Remus' hand for support and decides, for the first time, to speak to him telepathically. He jumps slightly at first but then a slow grin creeps onto his intelligent face as he listens intently.

I'm not sure what's going to happen, Remus, but I agree with you one hundred percent. A power beyond our comprehension created us. One day soon, the truth will be revealed. And not just to us. I'm positive our moms know what's coming.

Remus mindspeaks to his soulmate, finding the process to be as easy as drawing breath.

Cass, we're in this together. It won't be long before others join us. I feel it in my soul.

The two young adults turn eighteen and learn from their mothers they are actually Reji beings, assimilating human forms. Everything makes sense now. The pieces are falling into place.

Both surrogate mothers and hybrid offspring will join Mithra's efforts to convince other citizens, at the right time, about knowledge of an afterlife, no matter how far-fetched it may seem. Mithra began the Reji propagation when his seed entered ripe, female bodies. It is only a matter of time until their presence on Mars is much greater. That's the plan anyway. However, plans are made to be thwarted.

Former IVOSS president Ret. Lt. Gen. Peters returned to Earth with his lapdog Hamilton years ago. Devon McDonald, recently elected as president, now oversees the governing of the colony. His inaugural term coincides with an alarming increase in alien sightings. Shapeshifting red beings can be seen gliding over the harsh terrain, making no attempt to hide their presence. Reviews of live feeds reveal creatures with extremely hostile facial features set in overly large heads, their red, bulbous eyes show no indication of peaceful intentions. The sightings have been getting closer and closer to the living barracks. Why have they come and what do they want?

All launches and rover trips have been placed on an indefinite hold. Full lock-down protocol is in place. Earth's ASDF is advising immediate enactment of defensive protocols. IVOSS will forever go down in history as a site of sustained, hostile alien contact. It will not be pretty.

Inside the Hib-lab, which is close to Skyport, ten hibernation pods hum softly, enclosing courageous human subjects placed in a coma-like state under artificial means, their respirations and heart beats slowed to near death. Core body temperatures are lowered, in imitation of '"zombie" Canadian wood frogs, who miraculously avoid death from freezing by altering blood composition. Five males and five females aren't scheduled to be awakened for two more months. Resuscitation overrides can only take place via top-security password clearance.

Devon calls an emergency meeting of his governing council. He and the original Quantum One crew members have not forgotten the sighting of a huge spaceship when they first arrived on Mars. The one that was never followed up on. Could these most recent sightings be connected? Devon isn't going to mess around. IVOSS has several subterranean chambers, accessible by seven different passages, which offer life-supporting supplies for up to six months. It has never been used, although it undergoes daily inspections for preparedness. The decision is also made to maintain the hibernation study until further orders are received.

Chapter Twenty-Six-Celestial Posturing

Mithra addresses his troops from within Mothership Rejenitus. She presently rests within the deepest impact crater on Mars, Hellas Planitia. Cloaking maneuvers remain in effect for added secrecy. Additional Reji craft orbit the red planet, undetectable beneath clandestine sheaths.

Radiant residents of Rejenitus! The Syren has revealed the truth to very few species, other than ours. We have been instructed to lead the human race into the Labyrinth of Everlasting Life! Let us join forces with the mature hybrids on Mars. They have set things in motion already. The females who bore them are now as one with us! We will present our mission to all remaining citizens on the red planet. Assimilation can take place rapidly via visual imagery followed by mental cellular osmosis, transpiring within their brains. Humans call this hypnosis; Reji prefer to call it enlightenment.

They are a fascinating species, mankind. Young, impressionable, yet extremely skeptical. Sexual satisfaction is one of their greatest, albeit fleeting pleasures. I have demonstrated to the women that mental orgasms are infinitely more profound and last for much longer than pleasures of the flesh. The titillating truth is out there. Beneath inherent lustful desires, there exists something even more fervently sought after by this race. Knowledge. The knowledge they can somehow be reunited with people who have passed on after their brief time in mortal bodies. This is particularly true for one of the females. She longs to be reunited with a lost loved one.

A buzzing fills the interior of Mothership Rejenitus as loyal warriors listen to their leader expectantly, black eyes shimmering with admiration.

Some will be easily convinced; others will be difficult to sway. Although we hope all humans join the exodus, some may be unable to accept the enormity of the proposition. Decisions are to be made willingly. Any who change their minds will not be harmed. However, the opportunity for eternal salvation will be lost. It is a one and done proposition, as we know, per doctrines dating back to the beginning of time.

Within the Syren, memories of loved ones who have passed on before can be reincarnated from celestial limbo. An extremely convincing bargaining chip with which to entice potential converts. However, it requires the abandonment of all other beliefs. ***This*** *is the tradeoff. A blind leap of faith. Something they are already accustomed to for they seek comfort in individual religions which preach similar requirements.*

Images enter Reji minds of the familiar ring of deepest sable which encircles the Luxar Galaxy. It resembles a monstrous inner tube containing brilliant spokes of innumerable burning suns, waxing and waning. Bright omens of immense portent. Each star represents a steppingstone into eventual eternity. Star Rejenitus burns in the nucleus, firing mountainous flames toward a looming precipice. No matter how violent, the molten eruptions come to an abrupt halt as they get sucked over the event horizon's edge, falling into something so powerful it snuffs out stars in the blink of an eye.

In fact, Mithra is one of only a few Reji to return from the Syren's fourth dimension of time. It is a vast entity, able to encompass and preserve each and every conscious thought of any species. A wormhole of wonder, capable of enfolding worlds and wandering souls into bottomless depths.

Citizens of Rejenitus! I have witnessed the Syren! Your destinies are forever promised to carry on within it, after the completion of cosmic missions. The Reji general population is still at risk from waring races. Let us bring others into the domain of discovery! They will join us in defending the truth. Mithra floats overhead gesturing to the throngs with semi-transparent upper appendages.

We have detected signs that the infernal Xerus, our blasted enemies, have made haste to arrive here before us. There is no doubt of malicious intent, for their feeble minds cannot grasp the import of what we offer to chosen races. The bitter taste of being spurned remains quite pungent. Envy festers within their chests like bubbling cauldrons. Rejection is not something they deal with well. Be prepared for opposition. Spare none, for they are the scourge of solar-spawned societies and will gladly die trying to spoil our efforts before they gain momentum. We must intercept and annihilate each and every red-blooded Xeru!

While Mithra addresses his troops on Mars, Vane is addressing faithful warriors on Phobos, the largest and closest of two moons which orbit Mars. Named after the Greek god of fear and panic, it is an appropriate location for a portion of the commander's hostile fleet to prepare for pre-invasion tactics.

Xenith's forward deck is abuzz with incensed Xerus, flitting about with renewed vigor after their leader has promised pillage and plunder. First, however, mankind's rudimentary human AI collection will be sabotaged to wreak havoc and destruction. Vane's throbbing vascular system pulses visibly through his vaporous form as he speaks telepathically. Red irises of incensed Xerus dilate and constrict in rhythm with the commander's thumping heart.

Soldiers! It won't be long before we cast humans into a world of hurt! They have seen our spies on the outside of this fledgling establishment and have no doubt taken immediate steps to protect themselves. There is most likely a subterranean dwelling which they believe is unbreachable. It should be quite easy to take control of these child-level robots and then enter this shelter. I will lead an attack force. Your burning loins will be satiated in good time with ample flesh. First, we spoil this idiotic mission before others are brainwashed by its blatant lies. Use our signature paralytic gas weapons, Xerus! They will drop like flies!

Jericho, along with Doma and Mirt begin the war dance, circling overhead. Excited Xerus chase each other so quickly their iridescent bodies resemble a flaming pinwheel, appearing as one unbroken ring of burning red-hot metal.

Unbeknownst to Vane is that Phobos' sister satellite currently conceals something of huge magnitude. Deimos is over 23,000 kilometers from Mars, farther out than Phobos and much smaller. Within the Crater of Swift, Earth's Allied Space Defense Force has placed an ingenious weapon of destruction, a remarkable collaboration of thirty space programs, culminating in a weapon which has yet to be utilized. One designed to protect mankind's right to colonize other worlds. First come, first serve. The universal law of civilized races. A law broken by races who don't give a flying fuck for rules of any kind.

The satellite's obscurity makes it an optimal site for placement of the Planetary Defense Missile Launch, located on the bottom of this vast depression. Although compact, the weapon possesses target capability with pinpoint accuracy. Manned remotely, PDML can locate, lock in, and destroy targets within seconds.

Chapter Twenty-Seven-It Begins

Xenith's power, killed since touching down on Phobos, allows the vessel to avoid detection from manmade systems, and, more importantly, from Reji superior tracking capability. The time is right to impede Mithra's infiltration deployment. Mirt and Doma float within the warship's command hub, preparing troops for invasion, barking orders like a K9 on a hot trail. Incensed Xerus launch individual rocket pods to the outside of the IVOSS android charging area so quickly, they are unnoticeable. Accustomed to extremely hot temperatures, their bodies remain protected from the freezing cold within razor-thin thermasuits.

Reddish blobs bleed from vessels, pouring over the planetary surface like crimson oil slicks. Unlike Reji, Xerus cannot survive prolonged exposure to frigid elements. They gather beneath a low-hanging eave of the building just out of reach of security cameras. Pitch black, starless skies are pregnant with the threat of incoming storms.

Elongated bodies melt through the walls of the arena. Once inside, Vane uses a cauterizer to reseal any weakened areas. It's the wee hours of the morning. A vast chamber is chock full of humming, open-eyed robots, charging battery packs while awaiting final orders from a new senior programmer who floats before them. Live feeds of the room are blocked.

Vane exudes superior airs no matter what level of intelligence he is addressing. He must portray himself as an infernal mastermind, even though his top aides know otherwise. Mesmerized androids receive verbal input commands. Their internal components click softly as viral programming takes charge of sabotaged motherboards. Robotic fingers twitch, eyelids blink slowly, cyan eyes shifting below them. A nightmarish vision of things to come. Vane's evil voice and actions control them now.

"Greetings AI warriors! Xerus are quite eager to commence annihilation of this primitive colony. It's a pity humans have no idea about their sad fate. Each of you is to invade, attack, and destroy these weakling life forms, where they live and where they work. Remember, you take orders from me now and only me. Vane holds a master control panel in one hand, which he will utilize when he is not face to face with his new robot regiment, screaming commands.

"Kill all colonists by whatever means necessary. Take no prisoners. Finally, incapacitate any methods of transportation they possess in case some of them try to escape."

The Xeru commander laughs derisively. Plumes of red particles rush out nostril slits, enveloping his wobbling head in a gaseous haze. As usual, at least three grossly tortuous vessels throb beneath the shiny skin of his domed forehead. He can no more prevent it than he can prevent his insatiable desire for alien coitus. Blistered pustules break out periodically on pink luminescent flesh. The red planet's air molecules are not reacting favorably with his Xerusian exoskin beneath the suit. Boiling temperatures are preferable to this foreign chemical composition.

An electrical charge permeates the air. Each android echoes Vane's laugh with his own, irises glowing with demonic delight. A few can be seen fist pumping in the air. Imminent anarchy excites them.

"Congratulations recruits, you won't be needing a charge for quite a long time, if ever again. CARRY OUT ORDERS IMMEDIATELY! EXTINGUISH ALL HUMAN LIFE!

The doors to the charging arena fly open. Vane now commands a formidable force of robotic turncoats.

V awakes at 2 a.m. with an ominous feeling of dread. This morning, a brand-new crop hydration process began in the greenhouses. Her harvest production team predicts a marked increase in monthly yields from the upgrade. In fact, the doctorate she's always wanted is now hers, as she's been able to further her education, making the difficult decision to remain on IVOSS. Dr. Cortez has made an aging mother even more proud, if that's possible. Work projects can't be blamed for sporadic sleep tonight.

Her relationship with Devon is still going strong. After dating for years, they finally moved in together last month. V confided in him long ago about her inability to bear children. He had kissed usually private tears away, assuring her it wasn't a big deal. Veronica tries to focus on the way he accepts her for how she is, but tonight, her thoughts keep returning to a dark place. A place where a sixth sense takes precedence. She is the only female who remains rather untouched from the alien encounter. Yet, at times, she feels her destiny has yet to be written. As if she is perched on the brink of unfathomable knowledge.

V used to be the Digital Ouija Board master in her early teens. A gullible age, to be sure. Friends would stay for sleepovers, hunched over an LED playing board. Shades pulled down. Adolescent faces transfixed on the game. Voicing questions all young girls ask, believing the planchette moved by spirits more so than a desperate attempt to be noticed and loved. As she aged, Veronica realized self-love has to come first.

What the hell. Why do I feel like something absolutely terrible is about to happen? Shit, there's no way I can get back to sleep, now.

She reaches for Devon, who should be in bed next to her, but isn't.

Huh?

V sits up quickly, reaching to tap the touchscreen of a floating holomon, increasing its brightness. There's a note on his pillow. "Couldn't sleep. Didn't want to disturb you babe-you've been really restless tonight. I'll be in the observatory. Love you."

Great. I'm alone.

Live feeds display a view of the building's hallway, all the way down to the elevator doors which is pretty far away. V zooms in closer. Shock spreads over her face as she watches at least two dozen, blue-eyed robots walking toward her unit. They look enraged, and all hold something in their hands. Several break down doors in the corner apartments. Olivia jumps when she hears muted screams coming through the feed.

Flashes of bright light explode into the corridor. The robots are systematically going from room to room, laser guns firing and fists flying. One-track killing machines, given long life by Vane's malicious software. Something he's pretty good at. Android sabotage. Too bad he can't improve his own flight software.

Fuck me. Veronica cusses almost as much as Mike. *Why the hell are androids storming the hallways?* She checks feeds from more housing units and security posts. Robots are rioting everywhere.

They've malfunctioned. My gut feeling was right on. I need to warn people!

Veronica throws on clothes as fast as she can, simultaneously pressing a red emergency button on her wrist device the required three times. She screams into it. "Code Red! Code Red! Everyone to the underground shelter. The androids have mutinied! Take inner passageways ONLY! There isn't time to grab anything. I repeat. We are under attack! Leave now!

IVOSS has, of course, participated in emergency dry runs. This time however, it's not a drill. Once V presses the button, she receives one minute to cancel the preliminary alarm before it turns into a colony-wide piercing siren. Time stands still. She looks around her unit, dazed.

Get your ass moving!

An emergency bag gets yanked out from under her bed, prepared within the first week of arriving. Thirty seconds left.

Se me olvido una foto de mama. V rushes to her bookshelf and picks up the most recent picture she has of Isla, who is blowing kisses into the camera. Her heart wrenches. Will she ever see her mother again? Running to the kitchen, she moves the electronic fridge out of the way and sees the secret passageway door, protected with a keypad. She punches in a self-created code that gets changed every month.

"Password incorrect. One of three attempts."

What the hell. That's impossible. Her fingers shake. *Goddamnit—I have this memorized!*

"Password incorrect. Two attempts used. One remaining." The cold, monotone voice is maddening as fuck.

Veronica is beyond angry. She takes two deep breaths of air to calm frazzled nerves. At the last second, the revised special character that she had neglected to end with for the first two login attempts, pops into her head.

Punch the damn asterisk for fuck's sake!

"Access granted. Door automatically closes and locks in 30 seconds."

Veronica pulls the fridge back into place and then somberly watches the door shut, wondering if she will ever return to her apartment again.

Chapter Twenty-Eight-Confrontations

"V! Thank God you're okay!" Devon rushes to her side through the crowd of people.

"I was checking security in the observatory. The dome is supposedly impenetrable, but I ordered extra measures today for protection. Backup steel panels are fully in place."

"Good job." Veronica hugs him tightly. They've seen and felt the changes around the colony more than anyone. A charge in the atmosphere. Like something big is going to happen. Something inconceivable.

The underground shelter is abuzz with citizens who anxiously watch live feeds of androids, violently storming living quarters at ground and upper levels. This is unbelievable. Emboldened slaves have become slayers. Thus far, the only casualties have been in the apartments attacked first. Most people have been able to get to the connected shelters via secret tunnels, checking their names off on wrist devices for tracking.

"Devon, when I woke and saw you were gone, that was the fucking icing on the cake. I knew something was about to go down." V lowers her voice. "Luckily, I saw the robots in time to warn everyone. These shelters are going to be our home now—for how long, is anyone's guess. Knowing you are leading us makes me feel safer. I'm here to help, so please, let me. I don't want you to bear the burden of whatever the fuck is happening by yourself."

Devon squeezes both of her hands. He's just the man IVOSS needs at the helm.

"Come with me. In a locked conference room, Devon and V join members of IVOSS' governing council. A video message is transmitted to the ASDF, notifying them of the alien threats. There will be a delay before Earth receives it, as well as the reply to IVOSS. Surely scientists back home already know something is amiss from data breaches.

The newly developed missile launch system on Deimos is programmed to seek out any indication of hostile alien presence near the colony or on its satellites and will be placed on standby arming mode. It is capable of multiple mass destruction maneuvers with no radioactive fallout. Quick annihilation without residual repercussions. While the council members wait for reports, Devon keeps talking.

"I'm adding Dr. Veronica Cortez to the council. She will be in charge of food protection and distribution. All housing arrangements were prepared formerly. I want inventory updates on medical supplies and number of terrasuits in case we need to make a break for it. Also, a charged rover count for when and if we can access the situation at surface level.

The connected emergency shelters, blasted out at the beginning of IVOSS' construction, are partially made of indigenous rock located on Mars. They are gargantuan, affording enough room for twice the population. Pre-mined supplies of water from ice stores are available, flowing from an ingeniously designed aqueduct system.

A knock comes on the main door. Devon looks at the conference room holomon, surprised to see the rest of Quantum One's crew with the addition of Cassi and Remus, waiting to gain admission.

"It's okay," Devon says. When the group enters, he motions for them to take seats at the table. Without warning, a black, vaporous form manifests over Susan and Olivia. It appears different in appearance from the hostile ones recently observed. Mithra's apparition brings looks of astonishment from the faces of the council, including Devon and V. His facial features bear no malice. Only an inherent understanding of how humans think. A deep voice speaks to them, telepathically.

Greetings. Do not be afraid. I am Mithra. Leader of Reborn Rejis from Star Rejenitus in the Luxar Galaxy. Your human friends who just entered have made the decision to join our mission. This planetary colony is under attack from hostile aliens who go by the name of Xerus. Their relentless, albeit ignorant, leader, is called Vane. He is the one responsible for sabotaging robots who have been ordered to find and kill each and every one of you. Rejis come in peace to offer assistance and an escape from imminent death.

Veronica is looking at Mithra like she's hypnotized. His eyes are huge and unblinking, with deep emotion hidden in their depths. Why does this—thing— look familiar to her? Flashes of the prior encounter pop into her head.

Dios mio. ***This*** *is what's been nagging at me all these years. Those random voices I occasionally heard. The aching in my loins. Residual guilt. Watching Susan and Olivia grow increasingly weird and fanatical. As if they knew something was going to happen.* Her swirling thoughts don't go unnoticed by Mithra.

Devon looks at V, noticing her sudden recognition of the alien. He's stumped.

"It's ok, Devon. He won't hurt us." Veronica assures him of her trust.

Olivia speaks to the others softly. "Mithra speaks the truth. He has asked me to explain. It was **his** ship that we encountered so many years ago, remember? That's what happened to Everett. He was taken for examination. To lead the way for us. He lives on with other Reji. Please, everyone, don't be afraid. We want to offer you a way out of this mess. Right here, right now."

"We? Liv, what the hell does 'we' mean?" Nick looks at his wife with an increasing sense of betrayal. "Why haven't you told me about this?"

Before Olivia can reply loud pounding is heard on the back door which leads to an air lock passageway. Devon makes a quick decision on whether or not to open it. He decides only humans knock to get in somewhere. Alien fuckers go wherever the hell they want, whenever they want. He yanks the door open.

Mike and Janice stumble into the room. She's whimpering like a baby. The Sky Transport Team lead wastes no time filling them in. His hand grips a sword-like weapon.

"Those pussy motherfuckers need to be blown outta here!" Mike wipes drops of blood off his cheeks from a deep cut received at the hand of a rioting robot. He points at Janice, who is wiping her snotty nose with a tattered tissue. "The two of us live in adjoining apartments. She was with me at the time. Fuckwads stormed in on us. I barely had time to decapitate the first one with my Samurai sword before turning on the other!"

Everyone looks at Mike, their shock replaced with confusion by what he just said. He hesitates, holding up his weapon. "Well, it's not a genuine Samurai-just one I made in the metal shop. Before the ballsacks could jump us, I sent their wired heads rolling down the hallway. You should have seen them bouncing down the aisle, spewing gibberish out of twisted mouths. Their eyes stayed open— fucking dicks."

Good ol' Mike. Master of Swords and Swear Words. He finally notices Mithra floating rather inconspicuously at the other end of the room.

"What the flying fuck is that?" Mike's jaw drops open. Janice, having seen the Reji, frantically cowers behind a chair, dropping her crumpled Kleenex on the floor.

Mithra nods his head, sending telepathic greetings to the newcomers. Of course, it freaks them out. Before the Reji can explain one of the council members points to the largest video feed. What they see is absolutely horrible. A scene of unrelenting destruction. Crimson aliens circle above terrified citizens who are dropping where they stand, completely paralyzed by a dense, claret haze in the air. Mouths trapped in screams that will never be heard from vocal cords rendered useless. Crumpled bodies pile up on each other, ramrod extremities sticking out like stick men. Vane and his warriors have breached the shelters. The lethal fumes Xerus created are the only serious threat ever used to eliminate Reji. Now it's being leveraged against a much weaker species. The carnage is devastating.

Chapter Twenty-Nine-Mithra Retaliates

"Hey! The alien is gone!" A petite, mousy-faced woman glances away from the horror on the holomon. The others track her outstretched arm, one stumpy finger pointing at empty space.

Mithra has indeed departed. He's going to waste no time in retaliation for the lives that Vane has stolen from him. A dire message enters the minds of those he left behind.

Humans. Everyone but the Reji recruits jump again at the foreboding words. *Do not enter the main shelter area or you will be immediately killed by paralytic gas. Xerus seek to destroy citizens not only on Mars but Earth, also. I will take care of them, once and for all. Believe me, we are on your side. If you leave this room, exit by the rear.*

They look at each other. A few touch their heads in disbelief at this new method of communication. Is this really happening? How could things go from bad to worse so quickly?

"Everyone, have a seat." Devon's voice is dead calm. "I'm not sure who the hell Mithra is but my gut instinct tells me he can be trusted. We are in the midst of an unheard-of crisis. It will take all of us working together to figure out how to come through it alive. An update from ASDF should arrive any minute. In the meantime, let's check storage in here for terrasuits and food rations. I'm positive there are two rovers at ground level that most likely have not been touched. They have enough of a charge to get us to the Skyport Sector.

Mithra returns to Mothership Rejenitus. Her gilded exterior remains cloaked. She waits patiently within Hellas Planitia. The gargantuan ship practically fills the crater, silently waiting for orders.

Warriors! Mithra summons his opposing forces. *Vane and his insidious troops infiltrated the colony. Human-created AI's revel in the throes of murderous mutiny. Xerus have managed to breach underground shelters and have already annihilated many lives by deploying dreaded paralytic gas. Who amongst you is willing to stop this desecration of human life? Step forward!*

Every single Reji combatant moves toward Mithra buzzing like crazed bug zappers on a hot summer night. This time, they are within protective exoskin and helmets, both impenetrable from the gas.

We are, Mithra! Until we draw our last breath, we will serve you and the Reji mission!

The huge black orbs of their leader grow large with pride. He dons his own protective gear. Long bony fingers on his left hand hold a compact weapon.

It is my honor to lead you! Let us make haste and eliminate the enemy! It is known that Xerus cannot survive the cold. Utilize your cold lasers which Cygorg created. Kill all but Vane. His death shall come by my hand! Follow!

Within the conference room, the holomon comes to life with a message from the ASDF.

General Cordova is the acting commander. His chiseled face appears on the screen. Hundreds of sober employees man computer terminals behind him.

"This message is for IVOSS President Devon McDonald. Hostile alien infiltration has been confirmed. I repeat. Hostile alien infiltration has been confirmed. The Planetary Defense Missile Launch is armed and will be fired from Deimos in thirty minutes, after final parameters are relayed and programmed. Remain in underground shelters until further notice. Do not attempt to go to surface level. The colony, unfortunately, will need to be sacrificed to eliminate the alien threat. IVOSS' northernmost rocket launch site will be spared. ASDF will do everything in its power to use as little force as possible, but aftershocks should be expected. Again, firing of the missile will take place in thirty minutes."

All of the air gets sucked out of the room. It would be extremely easy to panic over events that are now set in place without the ability to terminate. As usual, Devon stays cool.

"Guys, we're going to survive this. The colony is for all intents and purposes done for. I'm sorry. Who knows how many poor souls have perished out there." He gestures in the direction of the main arena.

Devon looks around at grim faces. Several people pace the room. Olivia and Remus are trying to explain things to Nick in a corner but it's not going well. His face is livid. He's just been informed that Remus is not his biological child.

"Lies! You are off your rocker, Olivia. I knew there was something weird going on the way you've been acting this entire year. After everything we've been through. Jesus, how could you be this deceitful and manipulative."

"Nick, listen to me, please. I was planning on telling you tonight, but the shit hit the fan! I did this for all of us so we can live forever!" Ask Remus!"

The Reji being gently informs his adoptive father of his true origin but Nick recoils violently from the information.

I can't believe I let another woman fuck me over. Jesus Christ, this sucks balls.

Olivia tries to touch her husband, but he cringes away, leaving her and Remus standing helplessly alone in the corner. "Stay away from me-both of you."

Devon motions for everyone to take a seat again. Nick makes it a point to sit in a chair farthest away from his family who are now nothing more than strangers. He won't even look at them.

"I've just remembered." Devon looks around the table. "Ten hibernation subjects still need our help. We can't let them be killed after they've risked so much already. I need Dr. Dorfmeyer to accompany me so their vitals can be checked after resuscitation. Plus, a couple more volunteers."

Susan, usually timid in her outlook, has blossomed into a brave Reji masked in a human body.

"Of course, I'll go with you. We need to leave right now before detonation!"

"Nick." Devon walks down to talk to his friend who has his head in his hands. "I'm so sorry-try to have an open mind. My head is spinning, also. I know this is incredibly hard for you." Nick ignores him. Devon turns to address the group.

"I'm placing Dr. Cortez and Mike in charge until we get back. I'll do my best to update you." V rushes up to the IVOSS president, who suddenly looks like he's aged ten years.

"Be careful, Devon. Don't make me come after you." She hugs him tightly.

"Remus and are going, too," Cassi hops up. "Let's go." Susan looks at her Reji daughter with pride. Olivia embraces Remus before they leave.

"I'll try getting through to your...father." Olivia glances from her son to her husband, hoping beyond hope that he'll come around in his thinking.

The four volunteers exit by the back airlock door. God only knows if they will make it to the hibernation ward in time.

Chapter Thirty-We Meet Again

Devon pulls up underground schematics on the Segway's LCD screen. Time is running out.

"Map the quickest route to the hibernation ward via sublevel routes." He voices the command softly.

"Mapping route, arrival in five minutes." Dr. Dorfmeyer looks at Devon with a commanding air about her that he can't help but notice as they ride side by side. Remus and Cassi bring up the rear.

They fill Devon in on Mithra's underlying mission, which the Reji leader was attempting to explain before his sudden departure to face the Xerusian onslaught.

"It's already hard enough, dealing with a hostile alien invasion. On top of that, humans need to decide if what you say about achieving everlasting life is the truth. I can't focus on that, yet, for God's sake. Let's save the poor souls in hibernation, first. They didn't ask for this shit show. We are their last hope."

"Your destination is directly above you. Access the hibernation ward via your immediate right." Monotone notifications become maddening during emergencies.

"I see nothing that even remotely resembles an elevator or hidden door to a stairwell," Susan frowns as they all disembark. "Wait-what does this black switch do?" She flips it and a panel slides laterally, revealing a formerly concealed elevator. Devon notices that the doctor's fingers appear more elongated than before.

When they step into the Hib-lab it looks like the robotic mob has not broken into the area yet. Ten pods run softly, their displays flash ongoing biometric stats. Beneath clear, supposedly breakproof domes, five Sleeping Beauties and five Prince Charmings repose in near-death states, totally oblivious to the ensuing crisis, their faces slack, and devoid of color.

"I received the security code to terminate hibernation this morning. Remus, Cassi, watch for threats. Dr.Dorfmeyer, let's do this." Devon punches the code into the main control terminal. "Commencing resuscitation."

"Twenty minutes until detonation of colony. Seek emergency underground shelter immediately. Do not return to surface level until permission is received." The automated message booms through the lab's overhead speakers.

Eyelids flutter beneath pod domes. Breathing quickens. Heart rates gradually return to normal levels as tubes recede like small garden snakes into openings on the sides of the pods. A hint of color returns to cheeks. The occupants will be fully conscious within five minutes. What they learn when completely revived will be unheard of.

Well, well, well, this is indeed an unexpected pleasure. Devon and Susan jerk, turning to see Vane and several Xerus surrounding Remus and Cassi.

"Leave them alone!" Dr. Dorfmeyer lunges toward the Reji offspring but stops dead in her tracks when the warriors brandish paralytic gas weaponry.

I will give the order to release gas bombs and you will never touch them again. Step back from those strange enclosures. The robots who are now under my command will soon destroy them, along with whatever is inside.

Susan and Devon step away from the pods. Within them, groggy occupants continue to regain consciousness.

Apologies. Allow me to introduce myself. I am Vane, commander of star-born Xerus from Amorpheus. Vane throws his huge head back with what looks and sounds like a sardonic laugh.

You should know the name of the race that will end your pitiful colonization efforts on this cold-ass planet. Mankind could have picked someplace warmer. Vane snorts hot red plumes in disgust, then chokes on his own exhaust.

Ah, speak of the devil.

Boom! Double steel doors slam to the floor as a mob of droids storm the room. They halt their forward progress under Vane's command, their brilliant blue eyes unblinking and distinctly malevolent.

"Jesus Christ-they want to kill us." Devon exclaims under his breath to Susan, who now looks like she wants to rip Vane's head off. Her eyes have turned a bluish black and her skin has a gray cast to it. The offspring begin to morph also. Their hair falls onto the white tiles of the Hib-lab floor. Soft locks curl up like shriveled dead weeds, eventually seeping into narrow cracks. Devon tries not to freak out but his own heart is racing from adrenaline. So much is happening at once. His wrist device vibrates, he's sure it's V trying to reach him, but he can't respond for fear of detection.

Shit, I'm the only human in this room, right now. Backup would be great.

The Xeru commander's neck vessels pulsate from excitement. It seems as though they will burst any second, splattering crimson liquid in all directions. Jericho rushes in to join his scarlet-enshrouded leader.

Now covered in the thinning skin of human flesh, the Reji recruits scan the room for an escape route, but there is none. They give off a scent only detectable by Xerus. It causes Vane to shudder with anticipation, as do the warriors. What a pity their young lives will soon be choked off, along with these weakling humans.

"Fifteen minutes until colony detonation. Seek underground shelter immediately." Devon can almost detect a change in the automated voice as if panic is setting in, little by little. He surmises it's his own paranoia. Veronica must know something is wrong by now since he hasn't responded.

Muffled thumps cause everyone to turn toward the sound. The humans have awakened and are thrashing weakly against the padded sides of pods. Devon's wild thoughts envision a cinema director calling out, "Cut!", before setting up the next scene. Surreal, for sure. Imagination overload.

Colony detonation? Interesting. Not a threat...for us. More snorts, Vane is cracking himself up.

Mesmerized robots respond to Vane's subtle command, moving toward the pods ready to use whatever methods are necessary for complete destruction, weapons in hand.

Mithra, flanked by Zorn and Cygorg appear as if by magic . The Reji leader's eyes are an impenetrable shade of deepest black.

Stop them, Vane, or you and your henchmen will feel the cold stab of death in your fickle hearts.

Vane takes one look at their cold lasers and shrinks back, immediately issuing a stay to his command. Susan, Remus, and Cassi have now morphed entirely, their Reji transformation is complete. Devon's mouth drops open.

Somebody wake me the fuck up. If I get out of this alive, I'm definitely writing a book about it.

"Ten minutes until IVOSS detonation. Seek underground shelter immediately." The voice sounds even more insistent in Devon's hyper-tuned mind. He tries to move but his leaden feet are rooted in place.

Mithra, what took you so long? Have you come to rescue these rudimentary creatures? Vane throws his bulbous head back and guffaws. His eyes are so swollen they look like they will pop from his throbbing head. *Sorry to spoil your little mission of salvation.* He attempts to relay a clandestine signal, ordering the release of gas bombs, but Mithra's sharp vision intercepts the sign. Cygorg notices it, also.

Bursts of cold laser fire reduce Vane's faithful comrades to scarlet puddles on the floor. He chokes and cries out with rage, rushing toward Mithra who calmly turns his weapon on the incensed Xeru leader.

I grow tired of your endless schemes, Vane. Eat shit and die. Mithra discharges his laser toward Vane's torrid face. It explodes in a sickening spray of vermillion liquid that falls to the floor. *Incredibly satisfying.* Mithra addresses the others. *Now then, we must make haste to the observatory. Mothership Rejenitus awaits us. Dr. Dorfmeyer, please help these humans rise from their......coffins.*

Chapter Thirty-One-There Is No Ending

Devon watches what used to be a human doctor check vitals on the revived hibernation subjects. The Reji simply places an elongated hand on each individual so that data can transfer into its fingers seamlessly. All participants are helped to a sitting position while telepathic words enter their minds, immediately calming trepidation.

Suddenly, Mike springs out of the elevator swinging his homemade Samurai sword over his head like a crazed maniac. With one ferocious swipe he severs the rigid heads of all the robots who have been frozen in place after Vane's quick demise. Devon catches a head before it hits his face. For a split second he gazes into ACharles-1010's nystagmus-plagued eyes, the synthetic muscles going haywire from residual electronic synapses. A hinged mouth opens and closes, as if trying to speak for the last time but nothing comes out. Devon tosses the grotesque head into the corner, wiping his hands on his pants to rid himself of the disgusting sensation.

Fuck, I'm never going to lose that image.

"Take that, you droid pussies!" Mike is still panting from the effort of decapitating ten robot heads. He notices Mithra and the other Reji beings floating around him. Perplexed, he looks to Devon for answers.

"Dude, where's doc and the other two kids? And, why the fuck is there red muck all over the floor?"

Before anyone can explain, Devon presses the buzzing button on his own wrist device. V's face comes into view.

"Devon, we're coming up. We sent Mike before us so Liv and I could try to convince Nick to join us, but he won't budge. Trace amounts of gas are creeping into the conference room. We had to leave. Maybe Nick will change his mind. We told him there's a Segway available. This place is going to be blown to bits in only a few short min—

"Five minutes until colony detonation. Seek underground shelter immediately!"

"Fuck me sideways. We're about out of time here, guys." Mike looks at Mithra who floats calmly across the room. He relays a mindboggling message.

Mothership Rejenitus has been summoned. She hovers just over your observatory. These shelters will not withstand a nuclear hit, no matter what your leaders say. I have witnessed too many of their kind. You must trust me even though there isn't ample time to explain right now. Embrace the unknown. Right here, right now. Or else perish under horrible conditions. Remember, we sought humans out for a reason.

Mithra's prophetic words hang in the air as Veronica stumbles out of the elevator, followed by Olivia, Janice, and the remaining council members.

"Michael!" You're okay!" Janice runs to Mike, blubbering her eyes out.

"She's fucking emotional, but I love her." He tosses his sword to the floor, embracing his sniveling girlfriend.

"Three minutes before detonation of the IVOSS colony. Seek underground shelter immediately and remain there until further communication is received."

Fatalities, the result of Xerusian weaponry, continue. Jericho and Doma still seek remaining survivors, incensed over reports their commander has been assassinated. The shelters' occupants are dead and gone but there may be some humans who remain in hiding at ground level. Vane's faithful troops will have important decisions to make in the near future.

"Two minutes until colony detonation. Seek shelter below surface level immediately."

Olivia bursts into the room. "I tried and tried to get through to Nick but he is inconsolable. I feel horrible. But, if I have the slightest chance to be reunited with my little brother, I'm going to take it." She looks at Remus, not surprised that his transformation is complete. He approaches his surrogate mother and takes her hand in his. In a matter of seconds, Olivia transforms herself. Veronica and Devon are convinced that whatever is taking place is something they want to be a part of no matter how fucked up it appears on the surface.

Devon has no idea how they all make it to the observatory with a minute to spare. He punches in the sequence to open the steel backup panel and main aperture of the observatory.

Mothership Rejenitus hovers above, completely obscuring scintillating stars overhead with her massive golden girth. A chute unfurls from the lower deck of the ship, sealing the opening from harmful elements. Soft light, like morning rays from a summer sun warms the upturned, drop-jawed faces of the humans, who waste no time in agreeing to do whatever ensures their survival. More detailed explanations can come later. The Rejis float into the ship, moving as gracefully as butterflies floating on a lakeside breeze. Mithra takes Olivia's hand. She hovers at his side, Remus next to her.

"Thirty seconds until colony detonation. Seek underground shelter, immediately."

We welcome your arrival, brethren. The time has come to make final decisions. You can remain on this colony and rebuild what you have admittedly worked so hard to achieve. Or, you can join the Reji exodus to eventually discover the true meaning of immortality. I never said it would be an easy choice, for all decisions life forms make have consequences and reactions. When one door closes another shall open. Everything will be done to rejoin you with your loved ones in due time. Citizens on Earth await us. First, we must return to our home galaxy.

Devon looks at Veronica. Their minds are made up. Fate has stepped in via methods they never dreamed possible. They follow the hibernation participants up the golden plank, turning to take one last look at the reclined seat they recently made love in. The telescope remains aimed at the blue planet, her beautiful colors drift over fathomless waters and ever-changing continents, obscuring the frenzied pace of life below.

There will be setbacks. There will be loss of life. Mankind, with trademark resilience, will rise to the challenge. They will be unstoppable. They will be given choices to make. From other forces and life forms. But nothing will be like this. Nothing.

"Final warning. Ten seconds until colony detonation. Seek underground shelter NOW!"

The Planetary Missile Defense Launch on Deimos fires its missile, aimed to destroy IVOSS from ground level up. General Cordova, along with the Allied Space Defense Force knows that this is only the beginning of battling alien threats in mankind's efforts to expand their horizons. Efforts to reach the governing council are unsuccessful, communication suddenly lost in a quagmire of unreceived keystrokes. Mankind's presence on Mars is at serious risk of temporary elimination.

The chute recedes into Mothership Rejenitus. She drifts above the observatory briefly and then lifts straight up, making no sound at all. The ship trembles from massive explosions taking place on the surface of Mars and Phobos. IVOSS has been annihilated. In time, it will be rebuilt by new space pioneers. Each rebuild will be better than the last. Forward progress takes time.

Mithra speaks to them again. His deep voice washes over them all. Soothing yet determined.

There will always be risk from hostile threats. All life forms, including Reji are susceptible to certain things, like the gas Xerus use against us. Thus far, it has been the only weapon able to penetrate our defenses. I have severed the head of the serpent, at least for now. Welcome aboard the Mothership!

Devon and Veronica are still human. In time, their bodies will morph. V wants to return to her mother first.

She's gonna shit her pants. Nos vemos pronto, mama.

Olivia feels the presence of Shiloh surrounding her. She knows that eventually the two of them will meet again. Call it a dream state or even a super level of consciousness. What it is called does not matter. Only what will be.

The gargantuan vessel heads toward the Luxar Galaxy with an intense burst of energy from her nuclear engines. Where all mankind should be headed.

Into the sun.

Don't miss out!

Visit the website below and you can sign up to receive emails whenever Susan Draper publishes a new book. There's no charge and no obligation.

https://books2read.com/r/B-A-YIBO-BQIOC

Connecting independent readers to independent writers.

Also by Susan Draper

Cataclysm in the Cosmos
Virus Attack
Survival
A New World

Standalone
Into The Sun

Watch for more at suedraper.blogspot.com.

About the Author

Susan Draper blogged for seven years before she self-published her first book, *Random Reflections: Poems from a Hoosier Girl.*

Next came a middle grade fantasy/science fiction series, *Cataclysm in the Cosmos,* guaranteed to engage young minds.

Susan invites readers to partake in her writing journey, as she believes fiction worlds can transport us to unlimited destinations. Find her current stories on Kindle Vella!

Susan has been happily married to her husband for forty years. They have two wonderful daughters, great sons-in-law, and two beautiful granddaughters named Aspen and Autumn.

When she is not writing she enjoys reading, running, tennis, golf, and her beloved Chicago Cubs.

Sign up for email alerts on her personal website!

Read more at suedraper.blogspot.com.

www.ingramcontent.com/pod-product-compliance
Lightning Source LLC
LaVergne TN
LVHW012118170826
845678LV00014BA/2989

9798223453772